Detective Rachel King Thrillers Book 3

WRONG VICTIM

An absolutely gripping crime mystery
with a massive twist

HELEN H. DURRANT

JOFFE
BOOKS

First published 2019
Joffe Books, London
www.joffebooks.com

Please join our mailing list for free kindle crime thriller, detective, mystery, and romance books and new releases.

www.joffebooks.com

ISBN: 978-1-78931-274-4

For Layla, one of my gorgeous granddaughters,
for listening to my endless chat about the plot
of this one when we were on holiday this summer.

PROLOGUE

The moment he walked through the door, the smell hit him, a mix of vomit and urine that caught in the back of the throat and turned the stomach. Another thing wrong, no one was about. Surely, someone should have come to investigate the footsteps in the corridor? A quick glance towards the ceiling, there were no cameras either. This place was still in the dark ages. Well, he wasn't complaining, it suited him.

The room his victim occupied was one of the cheapest, tiny and equipped with the bare essentials. Shame about the view, nothing more inspiring than the wall of the block opposite and half a car park.

His victim was lying on his back, in a single bed. Asleep. His irregular breathing punctuated by the odd cough. He looked nothing like the man the killer remembered. He presumed that was down to the ravages of illness. The victim was pale, haggard, delicate, someone who'd require help to do the simplest of tasks. What he was about to do would be more of a kindness than a crime, he wouldn't last much longer anyway, not in his condition. This would cut out the suffering, stop the man being a burden to the staff, his family and himself.

The weapon he would use was nothing more alarming than a pillow taken from the end of the bed. The man wouldn't put up a fight, there was no strength left in those emaciated arms. It felt good standing here with his prey unable to retaliate, the best thing that had happened in ages. Was it wrong to feel this way? His mother always said he had a dark side. Well, she was right.

It was time. The killer placed the pillow over the man's face and pressed down hard. There was a judder of limbs, a stifled groan, hands flailed feebly for a few moments, and in seconds, it was over.

Satisfied, the killer replaced the pillow. They'd find the man the following morning, cold and stiff. But the nurse mustn't presume that he'd died in his sleep. She and the others who would come after her must know the truth. This was no accident.

Taking hold of the old man's left hand, the killer selected the finger with the wide gold wedding band. A quick snip with a sharp pair of secateurs, a tug to free the bone from the joint, and it was off. A fine trophy to start the collection. Now the final touch. Taking a box of wedding confetti from his pocket, he tore it open and shook it over the body. The tiny pieces of paper fluttered down like coloured snow.

The trophy was one thing, but let them make sense of that!

CHAPTER ONE

"Want to do this again?" Mark Kenton asked.

Rachel King gave him a thin smile and shrugged. "I thought we didn't get on?" They'd certainly struggled the last time their paths had crossed.

"True, but we shouldn't let that stop us."

He smiled as he spoke but his tone was laced with sarcasm. Rachel's first response was to refuse the invitation, but the opportunity was too tempting to pass up. DCI Mark Kenton's sudden interest in her was totally unexpected. During their last encounter, a particularly nasty case of murder and people trafficking, they'd been reluctant to trust each other. The trafficking case had been Kenton's baby for months and he saw Rachel's involvement as interference. But she had no choice, the murders she was investigating were mixed in with the trafficking.

"We start seeing each other regularly, people will talk," she said.

"Let them. I quite like being the hot topic around the office." He smiled again.

"As long as it's your office," she parried. "If I agree, shall we come here again? It does good food and it's a handy bolthole after work."

"See, I'm really a thoughtful sort of guy."

Rachel didn't believe that for one moment. This was a fishing trip, and she wasn't in the mood. "Thoughtful? I don't think so, Mark. You're after something. Why not just come out with it? It'll save us both a lot of time."

She watched him wrestle with this. He looked like he was about to say something she wouldn't like, and Rachel had a pretty good idea what it was.

"Okay, I admit I do have an ulterior motive for tonight," he finally admitted. "I wondered if McAteer had made contact."

McAteer! Rachel knew it. Kenton was obsessed. He wasn't going to rest until he had McAteer behind bars. Kenton had him down as the 'Mr Big' behind the trafficking, and he'd done a runner. Of the two other main players, one was dead and as far as Rachel knew, Kenton had brokered a deal with the third for information. "Why would he do that, Mark? I'm a copper and he's an ex-villain on the run."

"It's not that simple though, is it? He trusts you. After all, you were once lovers," he said. "You've known Jed McAteer for most of your life and you're still close, so don't play coy with me. If the man was going to contact anyone, it'd likely be you."

The night had turned sour. Still, two could play this game.

"Leonora Blake. Remember her?" Rachel threw back. "The woman you cut a deal with? She was the one who dropped McAteer in it, told you the trafficking was down to him. Shouldn't you ask her if she's heard from him?" She watched his face cloud. "You do realise, don't you, that whatever Leonora told you was a pack of lies? She said exactly what you wanted to hear in an effort to save her own skin. She played you, Mark, and though she was guilty as sin, you let her walk away scot free. Instead of obsessing about McAteer, you should haul her in. Get her to tell you the truth this time."

Rachel was tired of doing battle with Kenton every time they met. Ordinarily, their paths wouldn't have crossed, since

Kenton was based at the Salford station. But a month ago his investigation into people trafficking, and the two murders Rachel had on her plate became interwoven. His refusal to trust her, or allow her access to the suspects he'd arrested, had made for a difficult relationship. It had also led to her almost getting shot. Interestingly, he'd made no mention of that tonight. He'd not even asked how she was dealing with the fallout.

Rachel wasn't happy with the outcome of the trafficking case. She didn't like trade-offs, and the one Kenton had bartered with Leonora Blake was made all the worse by her shifting the blame onto Jed McAteer.

"You know that Leonora's reward for information given to us was her freedom?" he said.

"You've been had, Mark. Leonora Blake didn't help you, because she knows nothing. Whatever she told you was pure fantasy. You've got this all wrong. Jed McAteer was not involved."

"You seem very sure of that. I'd be careful who I put my trust in, if I was you," he said.

Rachel had had enough. "What are we doing pretending to be friends, Mark? We just waste our time arguing about something we're never going to agree on."

"But we are friends, Rachel," he insisted. "We have a lot in common."

"Friends, no. Things in common, probably."

He obviously didn't like this reply, but Rachel was past caring. While he continued to pursue McAteer in this blinkered fashion, she had no time for Mark Kenton. She'd accepted his invitation for tonight merely to suit her own ends. Initially she'd played the same game as him, wanting to discover if there'd been any developments in the trafficking case or in finding McAteer's whereabouts. Rachel could only guess at why McAteer had done a runner shortly after Leonora Blake had been arrested. But Kenton was making a big mistake in believing that McAteer had any involvement in the case.

But Kenton said he had evidence which, to Rachel's annoyance, he refused to produce. She decided that whatever he had was probably based on his research into Jed's dodgy past. Like her, Kenton knew that in his younger days, McAteer had been at the centre of criminal activity in Manchester and was guilty of many crimes. Rachel had fought his corner, explained that he had changed, put his past behind him. Insisted that he was no people trafficker. But knowing the sort of person Kenton was, he was unlikely to take that at face value.

He was the first to break the uneasy silence between them. "We should meet up again, give a date another go. Next time, we agree not to talk about work, or McAteer — and you can pay."

That made her laugh. "You're mistaking me for a woman with money, DCI Kenton. You ask me out, particularly to a place like this, then you pay. This is the posh end of Manchester and far too expensive for me." That was a dig. He was a DCI like her, so how could he afford to eat here?

Ignoring the jibe, he said, "How about the weekend?"

"Mean what you said about not quizzing me about McAteer and I might think about it," she said. "Kids allowing, of course." She was referring to her two teenage daughters. "You don't have children, do you?"

He shrugged. "I never found the right woman, or the time."

That surprised Rachel. He wasn't bad-looking once you got used to the close-cropped hair and thuggish looks.

"Anyway, what woman would want a selfish git like me?" he said. "I like my own space. Kids would do my head in." Kenton took the proffered bill and nodded at the waiter. "Better get you home."

"I can get a taxi, it's no bother."

"I've had nothing to drink, so I can run you," he said.

Rachel really didn't want this. She much preferred to keep Kenton at a distance — for the time being anyway. She was saved from any further awkwardness by the sound of her mobile ringing. Glancing at the screen, she smiled inwardly. It was Elwyn Pryce, her sergeant. Saved.

"Looks like a change of plan anyway," she said, accepting the call. She listened intently for a few moments and then looked at Kenton. "Yep, the night's well and truly over. Sorry, but work calls." Fortunately, she hadn't drunk much. "I'll get that taxi after all."

* * *

Twenty minutes later, Rachel's taxi pulled up outside Hawthorne Lodge Nursing Home. The house was a three-storey Edwardian detached, built of red brick. Rachel surveyed the property — old, draughty and a bugger to heat.

DS Elwyn Pryce met Rachel in the first floor corridor. "Butterfield is in there with his lot, and the room is too small for all of us."

"Stick your head round and let him know I'm here. What happened?"

"The bloke was murdered, there's no doubt about that. The killer took one of his fingers as a trophy."

Rachel shuddered. "As if these places aren't depressing enough, now the residents are soft targets for killers. I hope to God I never end up in somewhere like this."

Elwyn nudged her. "No chance of that."

"Who knows what the future holds. Seriously, Elwyn, an accident, or illness later on in life . . . people move into these places for all sorts of reasons, it's not their fault."

"Actually, our victim is a case in point. He's here recuperating after suffering a heart attack. Rather than leave his family to care for him, he checked himself into this place."

"He must have been desperate. It's hardly the Ritz, is it?"

Elwyn nodded. "The whole place needs work. Wouldn't want one of mine staying somewhere like this, but I suppose it's a matter of cost. It didn't take you long to get here, where were you?"

"In town, on a date with Kenton." She noticed the surprise on Elwyn's face. "Come on, spit it out! What's on your mind?"

"I thought you didn't like the man. After the trafficking case, you said if you ever saw him again it would be too soon."

"He asked me out and I agreed because it was an opportunity to quiz him about what he's found out since. Which is nothing, by the way. He's no idea where Jed is hiding and he won't say what he's done with Leonora either. Keep it to yourself, though, just in case anyone gets the wrong idea." She didn't want this gossiped about in the office. The quietly spoken Welshman was the only member of her team that Rachel discussed anything personal with. They were colleagues, but also good friends. Elwyn was her sounding board for personal and professional issues.

"You don't fancy a relationship with him then?" he asked.

"Don't be daft, Elwyn. I'm not sure I even like the man! In fact, your call saved me from the embarrassment of having him take me home." She shuddered. "I'm on a mission, as well you know. I want to know more about that trafficking operation and how he wrapped it up so neatly."

"That was weeks ago. Get the file out, read the reports," he said.

It was obvious from his tone that he didn't approve. It irritated Rachel that Elwyn was another one who believed the trafficking had been led by McAteer. "Can't get hold of them. I've no idea what happened to our prime witness, Leonora Blake. We made the arrest but Kenton whisked her off to Salford to interview her. Since then there's been no trace of the woman. It's as if she disappeared into thin air. She's never gone to trial and there was no guilty plea, so he must have offered her a deal, but what did she tell him in return?"

Leonora Blake and her husband, Ronan, had been involved in a people-trafficking case which the Salford force were investigating. Ronan had been shot dead and Leonora put into a safe house in exchange for information about the person at the top. McAteer had skipped the country and was now a wanted man. Rachel assumed because it was his name Leonora had given to Kenton.

"She gave Kenton info on McAteer in exchange for her freedom. We guessed that was on the cards, didn't we?"

Rachel glared at him. "She had no information to give. Anything she told Kenton had to be lies. I know Jed McAteer, and he'd never get mixed up in anything like that. He's skipped the country because he had no choice. You know the odds were stacked heavily against him."

Elwyn ducked out of her way. "Possibly because he was guilty."

Rachel let it go, she trusted her instincts. Many moons ago, when Rachel had been at university, she and Jed McAteer had been close. Had he not become one of Manchester's most notorious villains, she would have married him. But, given her career choice, that was out of the question. These days Jed gave the impression of being a reformed character, a successful developer with money and a new set of friends. Rachel was under no illusions, he'd done a lot of bad things in his time, but not what Kenton had him down for.

Time to change the subject. "Do we have an identity for the victim?"

Elwyn consulted his notes. "Francis Baslow, sixty-two, and a retired businessman. As I said, he was admitted here three months ago after he had a heart attack. Since then his health has deteriorated dramatically. That is down to him refusing further surgery. His doctors told him only last week that he didn't have long without it. He was on borrowed time, Rachel."

"Family?"

"His wife is dead, there's a son in New Zealand and a daughter that lives locally."

"Who found him?" she asked.

"A nurse, doing the medication round an hour ago. Despite the number of deaths they deal with in here, the horror of this one got to her. She's in shock and not up to talking yet," Elwyn said.

The door opened and Butterfield ushered them inside. "He's been dead about an hour. He was brought a drink about eight and the nurse found him at nine. Suffocated. That pillow at the end of the bed is our favourite. We'll get it tested."

Rachel looked at the dead man. He was painfully thin and as white as the sheet he lay on. "What's all that stuff over him?"

"Confetti," Elwyn replied.

"That's a weird one. Has anyone come up with an explanation for it?"

Elwyn shook his head. "His ring finger on the left hand is missing too. Not a particularly neat job."

Baslow looked very different from the majority of murder victims Rachel attended. Apart from the hand, there were no other wounds. There was very little blood. He lay on his back with the duvet pulled up to his waist, looking peaceful, as if a gentle shake would wake him. Rachel moved in for a closer look. "He didn't try to put up a fight?"

"I doubt he had the strength," Butterfield said.

She shuddered. "Poor man. Not a nice way to go." Rachel turned to Butterworth. "You can take him." Then she noticed a woman standing in the doorway. "And you are?"

"Pat Wentworth, the owner and senior nurse."

"What sort of man was he?" Rachel asked.

"I can't say I knew him very well. We've never actually had a proper conversation. He preferred to keep himself to himself, did Francis. We thought he'd be staying about six months, but as his heart got weaker, it became obvious it was going to be longer than that."

"Did he have a mobile or laptop?"

"He had a mobile. He used it a lot. I presume he was texting his son in New Zealand." Pat Wentworth opened the drawer in the bedside cabinet. "Here it is."

"We'll have to take this," Rachel said. "His daughter — where do we find her?"

"Julia Baslow. I have her address in the office, I'll get it for you. I don't know what she'll be able to tell you though. She's not been here once since Francis was admitted. In fact, his only visitor has been the local vicar, Gordon Sankey. He spent a lot of time with Francis because he was sorry that he had no visitors."

That set the warning bells off. A family feud? Was that why the daughter kept away? "Had there been any concerns about Mr Baslow recently? Was anything or anyone bothering him?" Rachel asked.

"I doubt it. This is a nursing home, no one here would do him harm."

"Well, someone did," Rachel said shortly. "What security do you have?"

"That's what I don't understand. You have to use the keypad on the front door to get in. Whoever did this must have known the code because they didn't ring the bell. Unless this is down to someone working here, but I really can't see that."

"Do you have CCTV?" Rachel asked.

The woman looked embarrassed. "We've considered it, of course. But it was either that or new bedding. We have a limited budget so we have make hard choices."

Rachel was well aware that the fees for these places were expensive, and couldn't understand why there would be a shortage of funds. "You might like to consider it for the future. Are you sure Mr Baslow didn't have any other visitors apart from the vicar?"

"There was no one else, and because of his condition he didn't mix with the other residents either. It was a huge job simply getting him up and into the sitting room."

"We'll still need to speak to them and the staff. The killer got the entry code from someone. We'll do our best not to worry anyone, but the truth is, unless a resident or staff member killed Mr Baslow, someone simply walked in off the street tonight and did that." She nodded at the body. "And no one saw, heard or was alerted in any way."

"Surely you can't suspect one of our nurses or carers? They are all extremely dedicated and hard-working."

"I'd appreciate a list before I leave, and contact details for his son and daughter."

CHAPTER TWO

Day One

The following morning, Rachel assembled the team and told them of the incident at the nursing home. "We have no obvious motive. He was a helpless, sick man who was terminally ill and unlikely to live for much longer. All the killer had to do was bide his time. I'm at a loss as to why he bothered."

"In that case, someone really hated him," DC Jonny Farrell said. "Stands to reason. Cutting off his finger like that — the killer was making a point. He could have just smothered him and run. But he didn't want people thinking the death was natural. He wanted everyone to know that it was a deliberate act."

Rachel nodded. He could be right. "Well done, Jonny. I think you're on to something. That means we trawl through Francis Baslow's past, up to the present, and that will take time."

"It doesn't explain the confetti though," Elwyn said.

"We'll need to dig deeper to find the answer to that one, Elwyn," Rachel said.

"What about the family?" Elwyn asked.

"You and I will speak to them. I've already tried phoning the son in New Zealand but he's not answering. We'll go and see his daughter shortly. If she's agreeable, we'll take her to identify the body, and then we'll stay for the PM. There's something odd going on in that family. I was told last night that the daughter never visited her father. Given how sick he was, that's not natural." She looked at the two younger members of the team, DC Amy Metcalfe and Jonny Farrell. "Find out as much as you can about the victim and his two children. Look at their work, their personal life as well as their finances. Anything fishy, ring me on my mobile. Whoever killed Baslow let himself — or herself — into the building, and it has one of those digital keypads on the door. They must have known the combination, which smacks of the killer having help from inside. If you don't find anything on the family, start on the staff at Hawthorne, see if any of them are likely to be susceptible to bribery."

Superintendent Harding had entered the room and was studying the photo of Baslow on the board. "I've spoken to Stockport. They have a DS if we need him."

Some time ago, Rachel had been promised another detective for her team. Back then, Harding had said they'd get a DI, but that had never happened.

"Thank you, sir. We'll see how things go first, but if we do become pushed, I'll speak to them."

Rachel went into her office to get her jacket and car keys, Elwyn trailing in her wake. "Do we know where Julia Baslow lives?" she asked.

Instead of answering, he nodded back at Harding. "He looks dreadful. Should he be working?"

Rachel wondered what to tell him. A month ago, the super had confided to her that he was ill with cancer, and had asked her to keep it quiet. The problem was, he was deteriorating in front of their eyes, and didn't appear to be helping himself. He had said he was going to retire but must have put that on hold, but time off would be a start.

"He's got prostate cancer," she whispered, "but don't tell anyone else. He's not ready to go public yet. But he looks so ill it's only a matter of time before the gossip starts. When it does, you've no idea what's wrong, got that?"

* * *

Julia Baslow lived in Clayton, on the outskirts of the city. The house was a large semi in a pleasant avenue.

"I'm presuming she knows," Elwyn said.

"She was told last night," Rachel said. "Not the detail, simply that Francis had died and that the death was suspicious."

"That's an understatement."

"Even though there seems to be no love lost between them, we go easy," Rachel said. "After all, he was her father."

Julia Baslow answered the door. She was in her thirties, dressed in the usual jeans and sweat shirt. "I know why you're here. Are you sure there's been no mistake? Your constable told me a little, but I can't believe that anyone would want to harm my father. He was such an inoffensive, helpless man, wouldn't hurt a fly."

Rachel and Emlyn followed her into the sitting room. "This is never easy news to deliver, Ms Baslow, but there's no mistake. I'm afraid your father was murdered." Rachel gave the woman a moment or two for the words to sink in. "My colleague and I are sorry for your loss."

Julia Baslow's face fell even further. "Well, I can't imagine who'd do such a hideous thing. He had no enemies."

Rachel watched her. Why no tears? The woman looked more puzzled than upset. "The nursing home told us that he had no visitors. Is that correct? You're not aware of any old friends, work colleagues or family who might have popped in?"

"He might have been only sixty-two but he didn't see much of his contemporaries. And there's no family other than me and Colin, my brother. Pat was right. The only people who saw him would be the other residents at the home."

She smoothed her hair. A nervous gesture? Still no sign of emotion. "The local vicar from Saint Pauls, Gordon Sankey, spent time with your father," Rachel said. "Do you know him?"

Julia shook her head. "That surprises me. My father wasn't the least bit religious."

"What did your father do for a living?" Rachel asked.

"Until he became too ill, he ran a business. He sold retirement homes, on a site in Cheshire somewhere. He would never say very much about it. It made money, but he always complained about how boring it was."

"Mrs Wentworth told us that you never visited your father. Why was that?" Rachel asked.

Julia Baslow averted her eyes. "It's silly really, but I can't stand those places. It broke my heart when he went into Hawthorne, but it was his choice, you see. You probably think me hard, but believe me, I'll weep for my father later. I hated the thought of him being in a home, but there was no alternative. This house isn't suitable and I'm out at work all day. My mother was there before him and I watched her fade away to nothing. I couldn't do it again. I found myself making any excuse to stay away. I might as well tell you, because you'll find out anyway. You see, me and my father didn't always get on. In fact, before he went into Hawthorne it was all out war between us. He told anyone who'd listen that he never wanted to see me again. He'd changed a lot in recent times. After he had the heart attack, he didn't want me around anymore. Apart from which, it wasn't easy finding the time to visit. I work shifts at the bakery."

Rachel thought this was a poor excuse, an attempt to cover a cold, selfish attitude.

"We need you to identify the body," Rachel said. "We're happy to take you now, to get it over with, and I'll arrange for someone to bring you home afterwards."

"Do I have to?" Julia asked.

"You are his next of kin, your brother is in New Zealand, so I'm afraid it's down to you."

"I must warn you, I'm squeamish. I might react badly."

Rachel gave her a reassuring smile which didn't quite reach her eyes. "Don't worry about that. It doesn't take long, and he'll look much as you remember him."

"I'll get my coat."

* * *

On the way to the morgue, Julia Baslow sat in the back of Rachel's car, silent, her eyes on the passing traffic.

When they arrived, Rachel explained the procedure to her. "You don't even have to go into the same room as your father. The technician will pull back the sheet and you can just take a look through the window."

"I've never done this before." Her voice trembled. "My brother identified mother."

"There's nothing to be anxious about. Me and my colleague are beside you." Rachel understood the nerves, she didn't like the morgue either, but there was a job to be done. "Are you ready, Ms Baslow?"

She nodded. Rachel gestured to the technician. "Take a good look and tell me if that's your father, Francis Baslow."

Julia stared for several long seconds, Rachel waited by her side, arms folded, growing increasingly irritated. How long did it take to nod your head or whisper an affirmative?

Suddenly Julia seemed to rouse herself. "I don't know what you think you're doing putting me through this, but you've no right! I should damn well sue you for the stress you've caused me today."

The outburst was totally unexpected. "Julia, is that your father?" Rachel asked again.

"No, it most certainly is not. I've never seen that man before."

CHAPTER THREE

"Please, Elwyn, tell me that didn't just happen!" Rachel said.

"Sorry, Rachel, but it did, and it gives us a problem. If he isn't Baslow, then who the hell is he?"

With luck there'd be something found at the post-mortem or among the belongings that would help identify him. But this man had lived as Francis Baslow for at least three months. How had that even been possible?

"That woman damn well knew. That's why she never visited him. All that rubbish she spouted — she was playing us," Rachel said.

"Don't jump to conclusions," Elwyn said. "We'll speak to her again once she's got over the shock. She is bound to be as confused as we are."

He was right. Julia Baslow had been dragged here to identify a body, thinking it was her father. She must have questions they were in no position to answer yet. "Before we leave, we'll have a word with Dr Butterworth and Jude." This latter was Dr Judith Glover, a senior forensic scientist and an old friend. "We're going to need her help to discover his real identity. Then we'll have another word with Julia, interview the staff at Hawthorne Lodge, and have a serious talk with

Pat Wentworth. We'll also need to speak to the hospital, ask what they remember about Francis Baslow."

The pair walked along the corridor to Jude's lab.

"Why the long faces?" she said.

"We've just learnt that our dead male isn't who we thought he was. He's been using someone else's identity for several months, and no one noticed." A little flippant but it about summed it up.

Dr Judith Glover shook her head. "How was that squared with the family?"

"Whoever he really was chose well. The son's in New Zealand, the daughter never visited and the wife is dead. Apparently there's no one else."

"You're talking about the body brought in from Hawthorne Lodge?" Jude asked.

Rachel nodded. "We're really going to need your help with this."

"According to his notes, he was admitted to the home after treatment for a heart attack. The home was recommended because his doctor had advised a period of rest. Given what you've discovered, you have to consider that the real Francis Baslow is still out there somewhere. First off, you need to go back to the hospital that treated him and get their side of the story."

Rachel nodded. It was already on her to-do list.

"Don't worry," Jude said. "We'll look at dental records, take fingerprints and a sample of DNA. If he's on the database, we'll find him."

"And if he's not?"

"Don't be so pessimistic. Let us do our jobs first."

She had a point. The voice of reason, that was Jude. "D'you know when Butterfield will do the PM?" Rachel asked.

"It'll be sometime tomorrow. I'll text you well in advance."

Back in the car park, Rachel tossed Elwyn the car keys. "You drive. I'll ring the station and see if they've got anything."

Rachel spoke to DC Jonny Farrell, who confirmed that what they'd found on Julia Baslow appeared normal. The information about her working life was correct. She didn't have a record, not even a parking ticket.

"The house she lives in belongs to her. She was born there and inherited it off her mother. Francis Baslow lived in a place of his own."

For the time being, Rachel would give Julia the benefit of the doubt. But what about the owner of Hawthorne Lodge, Pat Wentworth? How did she fit into this puzzle?

* * *

"What do you mean, he wasn't Francis? Of course, he was, he lived here for three months," Pat Wentworth said.

"Julia Baslow said it wasn't her father," Rachel told her.

"I don't understand. Francis was her father! Perhaps her grief has affected her." The woman's confusion seemed genuine enough.

"I want you to think very carefully back to the time Francis came to live here," Rachel said. "What he was like, who came with him, anything and everything you recall."

"I might not be able to give you much detail. We have residents coming and going all the time."

"Who brought him here, do you remember that?" Elwyn asked.

"He arrived in a taxi, straight from the cardiac unit at Wythenshawe hospital."

"No family members were present?" Rachel asked.

"He was alone. He said his son lives abroad and his daughter was working." She hesitated. "You do know about the rift between Francis and his daughter?"

Rachel nodded. "Even so, you'd have thought his daughter would have made the effort."

"Was there anything odd about his arrival?" Elwyn asked.

Pat Wentworth thought for a moment. "There was something I did think unusual at the time. Everything Francis brought with him was brand new, even his toothbrush."

"Did he explain?" asked Elwyn. "Why hadn't he got someone to pack a case of stuff from his home? I mean, his daughter could have done that."

"I've no idea, and I didn't question it."

"What about the staff? Would any of them remember anything about his arrival?" Rachel asked.

"They might. I'll ask them."

Rachel handed her a card. "I'll have to speak to them all anyway. There's the problem of the killer knowing the entry code to get into the building. Would you pass on what I've told you about Francis and ask them to wrack their brains? Any little detail they recall could be important. I'll let you know the date and time."

The woman looked perplexed. "I don't understand what this is all about. We've never had anything like this happen before. It's very unsettling."

"We'll get to the bottom of it," Rachel said.

On the way out, Elwyn said, "The hospital it is then. First thing tomorrow we'll speak to the ward sister, check the records, see if there is CCTV. He must have been there a while, so someone should remember something about him."

"It's a long shot. The hospital is very busy, and there's a high turnover of patients. And what if he wasn't there under the name of Francis Baslow? What if our victim was known by his real name?"

"I don't know if you've realised it, but we have another problem," Elwyn said. "We don't know who the intended victim was, Baslow or our unknown."

Rachel closed her eyes. "Brilliant. Just what we need."

CHAPTER FOUR

He'd been watching her for weeks, but Alison Longhurst was too wrapped up in her tedious little life to notice. She was an insular woman who didn't have time for anyone outside her tiny circle. She lived in Ancoats with two teenage sons, but no man. From his limited experience, he had learned that Alison was a difficult woman to be around. The poor bloke had probably thrown the towel in years ago.

She kept to a strict routine, leaving for work each day at eight and returning at five thirty. These days she did shop work, a more honest occupation than when he'd first known her. But there was no chance of finding an opportunity at the store, it was far too busy. Nights were his best bet. Her boys were often out so she was home alone. He'd been following the sons on social media and knew there was a party tonight. It was likely that they'd both be gone until the morning.

His planning was meticulous, as it had been with his first victim. He took no risks. He didn't want to be spotted near where she lived and later have some photofit appear in the papers. He'd wear a hood that cast shadows over his face and a scarf wrapped around his neck and over his chin. He would not lose this opportunity, it had been too long in the planning.

He'd strike after dark. Park up a few streets away and walk the short distance to her house. Head down, hood up, a man in overalls carrying a tool bag. No one would take any notice.

He could almost taste the excitement. This would be two down. His plan was working just fine. One way or another, justice would be served, proper justice, not that watered-down version the courts doled out. He gave the front door a sharp rap. She answered, and he felt the nerves returning. He avoided looking her in the face, casting his eyes down. Of the three, Longhurst was the shrewdest, the least easily fooled.

"Evening. I was passing, thought we could have a chat."

"You!"

There was real fear on her face. He was flattered.

"I've got nothing to say to you, please leave," she said.

"I can't, there are things we should—"

"If you don't go, I'll call the police."

He knew that was a bluff. There was no way Alison wanted anything to do with the police.

He pushed his way in, slamming the front door behind him.

"Get out! I'm warning you, I'll scream for help."

"No one will hear, these walls are too thick. Do you have a cellar, Alison?"

He saw her glance towards a door on the other side of the kitchen. Grabbing her arm, he pulled her towards it. This was easy, she was too shocked to react. He dragged her down the stone steps, flicking on the light switch at the bottom. The cellar was clean and tidy and contained only a few bits of unwanted furniture stacked against a wall.

"Please don't hurt me," she pleaded. "Tell me what you want. Is it money? I have some savings."

"All I want, Alison, is for you to die, but I think you know that."

He took a wrench from his overall pocket and struck the side of her head. The blow sent her crashing to the floor, but was not hard enough to kill her.

He dragged the semi-conscious woman to the centre of the cellar and laid her on her back. She groaned and touched her head.

He knelt down beside her, whispering, "I'd like to say I'm sorry, Alison, but I'm not. Not sorry at all."

Her eyelids fluttered open. She seemed to be trying to focus on his face. He was sure he saw a glimmer of guilt. Perhaps, finally, she had come to understand why things had to end this way. The poor old sod in the care home had known nothing of his fate, which had taken the gloss off killing him. But Alison Longhurst was at this very moment experiencing the horror of knowing what was to come. After all, it was only fitting.

He'd made a promise to himself. Night after night, he'd lain awake and when he did sleep, endured the nightmares, the memory of what these people had done to him. Planning his revenge had kept him going through the hard times these last months.

"Goodbye, Alison. You've no idea how much I'm going to enjoy this." Taking a blue cushion from his tool bag, he pushed it down over her face with all his strength. Fighting for breath, she rolled from side to side. Kicked out. But he was too strong for her. It took only minutes, and then she moved no more. He took out the secateurs and pruned the ring finger from her left hand. A last scattering of confetti over the body, and it was done.

* * *

It had been a pig of a day. The Francis Baslow case was a mess. As she drove from Manchester to her home in the village of Poynton, Rachel went over what little they had.

She had plenty of time, the journey home was slow. Even though the rush hour had come and gone, the A6 was still busy. At the Rising Sun pub in Hazel Grove, she took the right fork and headed towards her house. With any luck, Alan, her ex-husband, would have prepared a meal. Just as well he lived next door. Rachel was well aware of how much she relied on him, but how long that would last was anyone's guess. He did so much to help because of their two daughters, but he'd recently got himself a girlfriend and there were bound to be complications sooner or later. *But please, not tonight.*

Both girls were home. Megan, eighteen and the eldest, was working in her room on an assignment for university. Mia, fourteen, was having words with her dad in the kitchen. Rachel could hear the raised voices as she came in through the door.

She walked in, put down her briefcase and threw her car keys onto the kitchen table. "Why all the noise? I could hear you from the drive."

"Ask him!" Mia said. "He's totally unreasonable. He just agrees with Meggy all the time. No one bothers about my feelings."

Alan was obviously at the end of his tether. "Meggy discovered that she's been talking to some man on Facebook," he said. "Mia won't say who he is. I've tried to explain things to her, how dangerous that is, but this is the reaction I get."

The pair must have been arguing for a while. Alan was red faced, pacing the kitchen, a sure sign he was angry. *Oh God.* Peace and quiet, that's all Rachel wanted. A night on the sofa with a trashy box set and a bottle of wine. But by the sound of it, what she'd walked into would take some sorting.

"I've warned you about this sort of thing, Mia. Friends your own age, that's okay, but we agreed no adults. There are a lot of dangerous people out there who target young girls in exactly this way. Remember Alice Brough's dad and what happened with him." Rachel was referring to a nasty incident during a previous case, in which Mia had been kidnapped by a suspect. "Who is he?" she asked her daughter.

"No one," she said sullenly.

"So how d'you know him?"

"I just do."

"Do we know him?"

"You do."

She read it in Mia's eyes. The instant they met hers, Rachel knew the truth. Wherever he was in the world, Jed was in contact with Mia. Fair enough, she was his daughter, but neither Alan nor Mia knew that. One way or another, this had to stop. But how?

"Your father's right. Delete him. Any comebacks, I'll deal with it."

Mia King turned on her heel and stormed off upstairs. "That's not fair, Mum, and you know it!"

"Mia spends far too much time in her room on that phone of hers," Alan said.

Rachel could do without this now. She wanted a quiet word with Mia without Alan listening in. "They're all the same, Alan. They're the Snapchat generation. It's what teens do."

"Who is he then, this man?" he asked.

"Look, I'll deal with it," Rachel said. "Lay down the ground rules again. She'll toe the line from now on."

"Should I be worried? Is our youngest being stalked by some online pervert?" Alan asked.

"Now you're being ridiculous. He's a friend of ours, me and Mia's. There's no need for you to be concerned."

"Then why didn't she just say so and save us the argument? Is he someone you're seeing?"

What to tell him? "*Was* seeing, Alan, but not anymore. Mia likes him and he's no danger. There's no harm done."

Rachel left Alan in the kitchen and went upstairs to have a word with Mia, wanting to make sure her instincts had been right. Once inside the girl's room, she closed the door behind her. "Is it Uncle Jed you're chatting with?"

Mia nodded. "Before he left, we agreed that he'd keep in touch. We're not doing any harm."

"I know you're not, sweetie, but your dad doesn't know much about Uncle Jed. Has he told you where he is?"

Mia shook her head. "I asked him but he won't say, just wants to know if we're okay. Reckons he's having a great time though. Wherever he is, it's hot and sunny."

Typical Jed. Soaking up the sun on some beach somewhere, when he should be here, trying to clear his name. How was that supposed to happen if he wouldn't come clean about what he knew and help the police?

"Do I have to delete him?" Mia asked.

"No, but be a bit more careful from now on. And don't tell Meggy or your dad."

"Why won't you tell me about him, Mum? He likes you, I know he does, but that doesn't explain why he met me that day and gave me the necklace. It belonged to his mum, so it must have meant a lot to him. And why does he want to stay in touch if he isn't someone special?"

There was no way Rachel could discuss this now. "It's complicated, Mia."

"I told Ella about him. She knows him too. He took us out once, remember? We went bowling in Macclesfield. D'you know what she thinks?"

Rachel's stomach did a somersault. These girls were young, but they weren't stupid.

"Ella reckons he's my real dad."

CHAPTER FIVE

Day Two

The following morning, Rachel left for work before the girls were out of bed. She convinced herself that the statements waiting in her in-tray and the day's schedule took precedence over her personal life. But that wasn't it. It was cowardice, pure and simple. She was avoiding the conversation she'd refused to have with Mia last night.

Sitting at her desk, Rachel texted her daughter, reminding her to take her insulin shot. Not that she was likely to forget. Mia had learnt to be meticulous about keeping her diabetes under control from a young age. Alan was doing the meals and he'd be there later when the girls got home from school. Rachel closed her eyes. She had to put this one away for the time being, or it'd do her head in.

Elwyn Pryce wandered into the office, holding two mugs of coffee. "You look a bit rough."

"I didn't sleep much — family stuff. Can you believe that Mia asked me outright if Jed was her dad?"

She saw the look. Elwyn wasn't surprised. "Time to fess up, Rachel. She's growing up fast. How long d'you think you can keep this to yourself? If you don't tell her, McAteer is bound to find some sneaky way of doing so."

"How can I, Elwyn? He's hardly one of Manchester's finest, is he? The man's a villain, currently wanted for people trafficking. What will she think?"

"Not good, I admit, but you'll have to find a way."

"And Alan? What do I tell him?"

Elwyn sat down. "You were going through a bad time. You and Alan weren't right back then. He knows that."

"When he learns that he's not Mia's real dad, he'll never forgive me. I know him, Elwyn. Hating me is one thing, but what if he turns against Mia? I couldn't stand that. No, this has to wait until she's older."

"Alan brought her up. He's her dad, pure and simple. Forget the biology, Rachel, and tell them."

There was no time to respond. A moment later, Jonny Farrell knocked on her office door and peered in. "You're needed, ma'am."

The young detective looked pale and out of sorts. "Good news, I hope. Like it's all been a mistake and the body *is* that of Francis Baslow after all." Who was she kidding? Rachel knew this case was going to be a bugger to unravel.

Jonny hesitated. "Sorry, but that's not it. There's been another murder. It's exactly like the Baslow one — suffocated, finger taken, confetti. The lot."

"Where?"

"Local. Harper Street. The victim, Alison Longhurst, lived there with her two sons. The boys were out partying last night and only got back this morning. One of them found the mother dead in the cellar."

The hospital would have to wait for now, this was far more important. "Right, Elwyn, let's go and take a look." She looked at Jonny. "Are you okay? You don't look very well."

The reply tumbled out. "My dad had a heart attack last night. He's in Wythenshawe."

Rachel knew that Jonny was dedicated to the job and wasn't surprised he'd come in, but he should have been with his dad. "I'm sorry, Jonny. You must be in shock. You don't have to be brave, you know. You can take compassionate leave, it's not a problem. Just say the word."

Jonny shook his head. "No, ma'am, I'll be fine, and so will he once they've treated him."

But he couldn't be sure of that. Rachel didn't know a lot about Jonny's family but she did know that Bobby Farrell, his dad, had been a football star. He was now a wealthy businessman with a string of sportswear shops. From the snippets of chat she'd been privy to, Bobby Farrell drove his staff hard and worked like a Trojan himself. "If you change your mind and decide to go, that's fine. Meanwhile, stay in the office and continue researching into the Baslows with Amy."

"What about the interviews at the care home?"

"We'll deal with that later."

* * *

The victim's home was a large semi, one of a row of similar properties. "Do we know anything about the family's background?" Rachel asked Elwyn.

"I've had a text off Stella, there's nothing known. She is trying to find out what happened to the husband."

"How old are the lads?"

"Eighteen and nineteen, one's at uni, the other starts this September. It was the older one who found her."

"Poor lad. A sight like that will take some getting over. Is family liaison organised?"

"Yes, one of the uniforms is there."

Dr Jude Glover knocked on the car window. "She was there all night. No sign of a scuffle, but she does have a nasty-looking bump on the back of her head."

So she was caught unawares. "We'll take a look." Rachel nudged Elwyn. "Come on."

"There's no sign of a break-in, so he either had a key or she let him in. I think the latter's more likely. One of the neighbours saw a workman heading this way along the street at about ten last night. Come on down, I'll show you." Jude led the way down the cellar steps.

The pathologist, Dr Colin Butterworth, was busy examining the body. "This one wasn't as compliant as Baslow, she had to be rendered harmless prior to suffocation. Apart from that, there was the same MO, even down to amputating the finger and scattering confetti over the body."

"There's no sign of the pillow or cushion used either," Jude added.

"Are you saying the killer brought one along?" Rachel asked.

"Possibly."

"How are the boys? Up to talking to us?"

"Their aunt is with them, the victim's sister. They're all pretty cut up," Jude said.

Natural enough. "Okay, we'll leave them until later." Rachel turned to Butterworth. "PM?"

"I'll do both victims later today."

Back outside, Rachel looked up and down the street. "Long gardens at the front. It would be easy to walk to the door and not be seen. A lot of them have trees blocking the view of the road. We'll still need to do a sweep though, see if anyone saw him or noticed anything odd, and ask about CCTV."

Rachel heard a man call out, "Excuse me! What's happened? Are the boys alright?"

Rachel eyed him up and down. He was tall, heavily built and casually dressed in jeans and a T-shirt. "You are?"

"Len Partington. I'm Beattie's partner, that's Alison's sister."

"I'm not able to tell you much at the moment, Mr Partington, but the boys and Alison's sister are fine."

"Can I see her?"

Rachel nodded at a uniformed PC. "Go and ask, will you?"

As they made their way back to the car, Elwyn asked. "Why her, Rachel? Have you thought about that?"

"I've no idea, but I don't think he's selecting his victims at random."

Elwyn shrugged. "You don't know that."

"Gut instinct. It's bound up with the finger thing and the confetti. Something links them, Elwyn. We find what that is, and we'll have found our killer."

CHAPTER SIX

Rachel wanted to speak to the people at the hospital. She left Elwyn at the station researching Alison Longhurst's past and took Jonny with her. It meant that Jonny could see his father.

"We're off to Wythenshawe," she said, "so you can check on your dad while we're there. You must be worried."

"I'm fine, ma'am. He'll have the operation and be back to normal as soon as. He's a strong man but he's a workaholic. The problem with him is he doesn't know when to call it a day. This might be the wake-up call he needs."

"Elwyn told me that he's badgering you to join him in the business."

Jonny shook his head. "That'll never happen. It's his thing, not mine. This is what I want to do. Dad can keep his little empire to himself."

He sounded adamant. Rachel wasn't sure how to react. "But if he needs you? Don't you feel torn?" Rachel had lost her parents in a car crash. Their absence these last years had left a huge hole in her life. If her dad had ever needed her, she'd have been at his side in a flash.

"He's a selfish git. He just wants to go on to his friends about how I'm like him and following in his footsteps. I don't want any part of it."

A touchy subject, evidently. "Okay, I'll drop it."

Wythenshawe was half an hour away from the station. Pulling into the car park, Rachel checked the time and found it was already gone two in the afternoon. Jude hadn't texted about the post-mortems, so she'd ring her in a while. The morgue could be their next stop.

Wythenshawe hospital specialised in cardiac cases. The ward where Francis Baslow had been treated was on the third floor.

They made their way up the stairs, Jonny reminding her that they hadn't got a warrant.

"I'm hoping they'll answer some general questions. We don't need to know any clinical details. The man is dead after all. Look, I'll be okay with this, why not take five minutes with your dad?"

"If you're sure," Jonny said. "I won't stay long, and I'll meet you back here."

The ward sister greeted Rachel — reception downstairs had told her they were coming. "I've had a look at the admission record for Francis and as it happens, I do remember him. He was a quiet chap, had very few visitors."

"Do you recall exactly who came to see him?" Rachel asked.

"That's simple enough — no one. His son is in New Zealand and he'd fallen out with his daughter. I believe they'd had a dreadful row just before Francis became ill, and he'd virtually disowned her. He made me promise not to let her near him. I've no idea what they argued about — he was tight-lipped about it. He spent his time chatting to the other patients, one Joseph Wignall in particular. I did warn Francis not to get too close. Wignall was an ex-con, and he made no secret of the fact he'd been in Strangeways."

Rachel was surprised. "And they got on?"

The sister nodded to a table in the centre of the ward. "Sat there and played cards most days. What they found to talk about is a mystery. They were from different worlds."

While they spoke, Jonny returned. "Dad's having a scan. I'll wait until visiting hours."

"Did Wignall have many visitors?" Rachel asked the sister.

"A young man, who said he was his son. I believe he had a sister too, but she never came near. He did have one visitor who wasn't family. A creepy-looking bloke. Huge, he was, bald and with a nasty-looking scar down one cheek. From his accent I'd say he was foreign. I didn't like the look of him or appreciate his attitude, so I had security on standby just in case."

Jonny seemed to start. The description rang a bell. He'd come up against someone exactly like that recently, during the trafficking case. "If I show you a photo, d'you think you might recognise him?"

Rachel stared at him. "What are you thinking?"

Jonny was busy texting Stella at the station. He looked up. "Vasile Danulescu?"

Rachel shook her head. Most unlikely. What was Jonny playing at? Danulescu was part of a trafficking gang they'd investigated about a month ago and wouldn't have anything to do with their present case. The young DC had had a bad experience at the thug's hands, but he had to let it go. "It won't be him, Jonny, and anyway the man is dead, he was shot right in front of me."

"Three months ago, ma'am, he was very much alive," he reminded.

This was wasting time. "Jonny, you have to drop this. He attacked you, but you got away. He's dead now and he can't harm you or anyone else anymore."

Jonny said nothing. Seconds later his mobile beeped and he showed the image on the screen to the nurse. "This him?"

Rachel couldn't believe the sister's response. "Yes, that's him. How did you know? I'm impressed."

She wasn't the only one. Rachel had mistakenly thought this was Jonny having some sort of PTSD. What did the Romanian thug want with a patient here? "I apologise," she said. "Your instincts were spot on, Jonny. But I'm confused. What can possibly connect Joseph Wignall and that villain?"

"Wignall may have been part of the ring, ma'am," Jonny offered.

"Possibly but he was far too ill to have been much use."

"He only came the once," the nurse said. "He and Wignall exchanged a few words and then he left."

"Do you know if he gave Wignall anything, a mobile for example?" Rachel asked.

"I couldn't say. Like most patients, Wignall had one. He used it all the time."

Rachel had no idea what this new information meant, if anything. A trafficking ring like that was bound to have minor criminals on the periphery. There was probably a logical explanation. "Tell me what happened when Francis left here," Rachel asked.

"Wignall rang for a taxi to take him home. Francis too, as I recall."

"Was that on the same day?"

"Yes, they more or less left together," the nurse said.

Rachel's eyes narrowed. "Was Wignall still poorly when he left?"

"I'm not allowed to divulge details like that."

"Okay, I understand. Don't give us any specifics, just tell us in general terms. Would he have survived for long, given his condition?"

"No, that much I will say. He could barely walk the length of the ward, I remember. We put him in a wheelchair to get him downstairs to the entrance. What he needed was extensive surgery, but he refused. Without it, his days were numbered, I'm afraid. Wignall needed the services of a nursing home far more than Francis, but he couldn't afford the fees. He assured us that his family were only too happy to take on his care."

"Did you speak to them about that?" Rachel asked.

"No, but Joseph said his sister lived close by and would help."

"Do you remember which taxi firm they used?"

"Bolton's, they're local."

"Will you arrange for us to have a copy of the CCTV from the exit the two men used that day?"

"It might take a day or so," the nurse said. "I'll need to sort it with security."

"Thank you. Email it over when it's ready. You've been a great help."

* * *

There was still no word from Jude or Butterfield about the PMs. Once she was back in her office, Rachel rang her.

"Dr Butterfield's been called away, so it'll be in the morning now," Jude explained. "But I do have something. I checked the database for prints and DNA and found a match for the Hawthorne Lodge body."

"Joseph Wignall," Rachel said.

"Yes. How did you find out so soon?"

"Wignall was in hospital at the same time as Baslow. For reasons I'm still puzzled about, I think they changed places when they left. Wignall went to Hawthorne and Baslow . . . well, I've no idea. And how they actually carried out the swap is a mystery too. I'll have to speak to the taxi firm he used."

The tasks were mounting up. Rachel joined the team in the incident room. "Longhurst. What have we got?"

"She's had her fair share of financial problems," Elwyn told her. "She's had a number of jobs but never stuck at any of them for very long. She bought into a number of businesses which all failed as well."

"What sort?"

"She had a share in a small corner shop, which folded after a couple of years. Then she bought a dog-grooming parlour. It went bust, leaving her with a mountain of debt."

"Dig a bit deeper," Rachel said. "Find out if she was held responsible for the failure of any of those businesses. Find out who the other shareholders were too. I've got an update on the first victim," she told the team. "The dead man from the home is one Joseph Wignall and not Francis Baslow at all. Wignall was a small-time crook who'd spent time inside. He was in hospital at the same time as Baslow, and the two became friends. Whether they planned between them to change places, or this arrangement was forced on Baslow, we don't know." She paused for a moment. "Wignall had few visitors, but one of them turns out to have been Vasile Danulescu." She saw the surprise on their faces. "Yes, I didn't believe it either at first, but DC Farrell showed the nurse a photo, and she confirmed that it was him."

"Does that mean Wignall was mixed up in the trafficking case, ma'am?" asked Amy.

"I don't know, but it's high on my list to find out. Was Wignall scared and in hiding, and took Baslow's place in the hope he wouldn't be found? It's understandable. Members of that ring were going down like flies at one time. I want all we can find on the man — his record, home address and those of his family members. The nurse on the ward said he had a sister and a son, neither have yet been told about his death."

"How was Baslow persuaded to go along with the plan?" Amy asked. "It's a big deal, changing places with someone and hoping to get away with it."

"We don't know that he did agree. We've no idea what happened to Baslow. For all we know, he could be dead too."

CHAPTER SEVEN

Rachel knocked on Harding's office door and given the late hour, was surprised to see him still hard at it.

"Damn paperwork, Rachel," he said with a wry smile. "I'm trying to clear my desk."

"You're taking time off, sir?"

"The NHS have done all they can for me, so I'm having a course of treatment in the States. Initially it will be pills and drawing up a treatment plan. I will be away for a few days, that's all," he said.

That was good news. The man looked dreadful. He should accept medical intervention while it was still an option.

"Perhaps then you'll retire, sir. Get over the op without the stress of this place?"

"Yes, I probably will, but I have to get the treatment done with first. An oncologist in California has developed something new and it's very successful. He's seen my notes and assures me he can help."

"That's wonderful news, sir. But won't it be expensive?" Rachel could have bitten her tongue. What was she doing discussing money with the superintendent?

He smiled. "There won't be a problem. Now, what can I do for you?"

"I need access to the files of the Blake case." He looked at her, his face blank. "You remember, sir, the people-trafficking case from a month ago."

"May I ask why, Rachel?"

"It is linked to a victim in my current case and I need the file to work out how. I've tried to download it off the system but I had no luck, and the physical paperwork hasn't been filed in the archives either."

"Have you spoken to Kenton? The case is still open so he'll have the paperwork."

"If you don't have access I'll have to, but perhaps you could have a word. I expect Kenton will be difficult about the matter. There are, er, trust issues between us."

Harding pulled a face. "He has trust issues with everyone, Rachel, not just you. He seems to think he can solve all of Greater Manchester's crimes on his own. Leave it with me, and I'll see what I can do. But I don't have much time, I'm flying tomorrow afternoon. You might just have to speak to the man yourself and persuade him to see reason."

"Will we have a stand-in, sir, while you're gone?" Rachel asked.

"I believe so," Harding said. "I'm told the individual is good and shouldn't give the teams in this station any problems."

Rachel wondered if she knew him. It was quite possible, and could turn out to be problematic. By and large, she didn't have much time for her counterparts in the local force.

"Do you know who it is?" she asked.

Harding shook his head. "All I know is that he's been appointed and confirmed. I'm sure it will be fine, Rachel. You've got a good team."

* * *

Rachel returned to her office, wondering how to get Kenton to hand over that file. He'd refuse if she asked. McAteer was on the run, meaning the case was still active, so he'd make up some excuse about still working on it. It was time to pack up for the night, but Kenton wasn't the only one with a sneaky streak, so before she left for home, she decided to try something. She rang him at the Salford station.

"Hi, Mark. Still want to take me out for dinner?"

"Why not? How are you fixed for the weekend?" He didn't sound surprised. In fact, he was suspiciously keen.

"I was thinking tomorrow," she said. "Me and the girls have something planned for the weekend." This was a lie — she had nothing planned.

"Okay. Want to go to the same place?" he said.

"Fine by me," she said, "but remember, I'm not paying. The prices in that restaurant are extortionate."

"My treat then."

"Pick me up from the station at about seven. I'll be waiting."

Kenton was a crafty sod, and since coming straight out with it was unlikely to work, she'd have to try something else. Phone call over, she went to the incident board and wrote Joseph Wignall's name in large capitals, circling it in red marker pen. Kenton couldn't possibly miss it when he came to pick her up. If the name was familiar to him from the trafficking case file, he'd have to mention it, he wouldn't be able to contain his curiosity. Rachel might not agree, but he saw the case as his. It had overlapped with one of her own before, and now it looked as if it might do so again. Kenton would talk to her or he'd get nothing more, and Harding wouldn't be here to stick up for him this time.

* * *

Rachel decided to call in on Julia Baslow on her way home. She wanted answers, at the very least a plausible explanation as to why she'd never visited her father in the nursing home.

Julia greeted Rachel brusquely, obviously not happy to see her. "I told you, that man in the morgue wasn't my father, so this murder you're investigating has nothing to do with me."

"It's not that simple," Rachel said. "You thought he *was* your father."

"I didn't know any different, did I? I believed my father was recuperating in that place and that he was doing well. I did ring Mrs Wentworth regularly to ask about him, and she gave me no cause to think otherwise."

"She never told you how fast he was deteriorating?" Rachel said.

"No, but I thought he'd probably told her not to."

"Given the ill-feeling between you, I understand that, but didn't you even once consider popping in yourself and having a word with him?"

"He wouldn't have liked that, and it would have set his recovery back. I've already told you we didn't get on. A huge rift had developed between us lately, and there was no way it could be breached. After my mother died, Dad thought he should inherit this house — it had been their home for decades. But it belonged to my mother and hers was the only name on the deeds. She had stated quite specifically in her will that it should come to me. He was furious when he found out. He admitted that if he had inherited, he would have sold the place. My mother would have turned in her grave."

"Who paid the nursing home fees?" asked Rachel.

"Dad did. The money came out of his account each month."

"You're sure?"

"Yes, I check the account online. We might have been at loggerheads, but he still trusted me. His eyesight was bad, so he gave me his log-in details and I make sure the bills are paid each month."

"In that case, he was paying the fees for a complete stranger, Ms Baslow. Doesn't that make you angry?" Rachel said.

"Yes, it damn well does, and it'll annoy Colin too. My brother and I are the sole heirs to my father's estate. We've wasted thousands on those fees. When you find out who that man's family are, I want compensating." She stared at Rachel. "What are you doing to find my father? He's not dead, therefore he's missing. Surely that is something you should investigate urgently."

"Believe me, we're doing exactly that. We need to speak to him about the man who took his place." Rachel took a moment to weigh the woman up. Julia Baslow did outrage well, she gave her that. Rachel was a shrewd judge of character, and she believed most of what the woman had said. But Julia was holding something back.

"Have you ever heard the name Joseph Wignall?" Rachel asked.

"No."

Did the reply come too fast? Rachel was about to question her further but changed her mind. She'd leave it for another time.

"Inspector, you have to understand that my father was a difficult man. I upset him and as far as he was concerned, that was that. Things would never be the same between us. It was a shame. But I couldn't let him take this house, it's not what my mother wanted."

"Did Pat Wentworth mention any other people who visited your father?"

"No, just the local vicar. My father was hard to get on with, hard to like really. He was bad-tempered and always had to have his own way. But I'm glad he had someone around. I know he contacted Colin by text, but how Colin responded I couldn't say. You'll have to ask him."

"Our people will speak to him. Did your father live alone before he became ill?"

"Yes, just a few streets away, although I rarely saw him."

"Do you have access to his house?" Rachel asked.

"Yes, I pop in regularly, pick up his post and make sure everything is okay. Nothing's changed since the ambulance carted him off to hospital."

"You're sure he's not been back? Are his clothes still where they were, for instance?"

"Nothing has been touched," Julia said.

"Okay, but I'm going to need the keys. My forensic colleagues will do a search."

Julia gave her a set from the hall table. "Keep me updated on my father. The minute you find him, I want to know."

Rachel handed Julia her card. "If you recall anything else, ring me."

CHAPTER EIGHT

Day Three

A jubilant DC Amy Metcalfe addressed the team the following morning. "I think I've found the link. As we know, the last failed business Alison Longhurst worked for was a company called Woodsmoor Investments Ltd. The company was registered at an address in Cheshire, and the owner of that property is listed as Francis Baslow. He was one of three partners and owned the lion's share, but he never actually worked in the company. The other two were Longhurst and a man called Samuel Graham."

"The business folded, you say?" Rachel asked.

Amy consulted her notes. "Yes, after only six months."

"And it was about investments, not weddings?" Jonny asked. "Only I'm still trying to make sense of the confetti."

"I'm not sure what the nature of the business was, I'm still researching that," Amy said.

"Cheshire? If it was a big country house, weddings would make more sense," Jonny added. "Make our job easier too. We'd be looking for a disgruntled customer and not some weirdo with a thing for confetti."

Too flippant, but given the stress he was under, Rachel let it pass. "Well done, Amy. I want you to find out as much as you can about Woodsmoor and that working partnership. Did Baslow and Longhurst part on good terms, and what became of Graham?"

"The problem I have there, ma'am, is that there is no one to ask. Alison Longhurst seems to have worked alone mostly. Baslow was very much in the background. At one point there was half a million in the company account, but that was cleared out three months ago."

"About the time Baslow disappeared," Rachel remarked.

"As for Samuel Graham, he's disappeared off the face of the earth. I rang the address we have for him and spoke to his wife. She wasn't very helpful — said he was working away and couldn't be reached."

"What do we think, team? Is this down to a disgruntled customer, or is it an inside job?" Rachel asked.

"That's what I'm trying to work out," Amy said. "But I've not managed to find anyone who had dealings with Woodsmoor yet."

"Keep trying, Amy. We need to know what that business was about and what sort of experience their customers had in dealing with it."

While Rachel had been speaking to Amy, Elwyn had been talking on the office phone.

"Jude's been on," he said. "The PMs for Wignall and Longhurst are set for this afternoon."

"We'll go, but first I need a word with digital forensics about Wignall's mobile phone."

"They're working on it. They're looking at both his calls and his search history. We have been promised a report today."

"Given that Alison Longhurst is dead too, and that they knew each other, I reckon that Baslow was the intended victim and not Wignall. We need to find out what happened to Baslow. For all we know, he could be out there living a new life."

"How? He's left everything behind," Elwyn said. "He owns property — it's lying empty. I had his bank account checked, and apart from the nursing home fees, it's not been touched, and there is money in it. He's been out of hospital for three months — he can't be living on fresh air."

Elwyn had a point. But what if it was Baslow who'd cleared out the Woodsmoor account? If so, he'd have more than enough to start a new life. Rachel wished she knew what the pair of them had been up to. Why had Wignall and Baslow swapped identities? If Wignall was afraid and needed to go into hiding, he could have had Baslow killed. He certainly knew the right people.

"No Harding this morning," Elwyn noted.

"He's gone to the US for treatment," Rachel said, and made a face. "We're getting a stand-in. Can't wait."

"What's the betting it'll be some high-flying DCI promoted for the duration? Any guesses?"

"I haven't thought about it much," she said. "All I know is that they didn't ask me. Should I feel miffed?"

"Grateful, more like. You'd hate being cooped up in that office all day, ploughing through paperwork. Leave it to the overly keen individual they've conned into it."

The team's information officer, Stella, handed Rachel a sheaf of papers. "All the details you asked for, everything I can find on Wignall. His sister's address is on the front page."

"We'll go and talk to her," Rachel said. "She lives in Longsight, just round the corner."

"We'll have to break the bad news," Elwyn said. "There's a son too. Do we know how old he is?"

Rachel looked at the notes. "Twenty-five. No mention of where he lives. We go easy, Elwyn. Wignall wasn't reported missing and I'm wondering if his family know the truth about what he was involved in. Did he tell them about his illness and the nursing home, for instance? If he didn't, this will come as a shock. His sister will have to identify the body."

* * *

The house was part of a terrace on a cobbled street behind the main road that ran through Longsight. All the properties were in dire need of work. The old wooden window frames were rotting and the paintwork had flaked off, exposing the bare wood. There was a small front garden, bordered by a low brick wall that looked as if someone had given it a good kicking. Loose bricks lay littered across the unkempt grass.

"What's the betting they all have the same landlord?" Elwyn said as they pulled up. "I'm sure there are laws against allowing folk to live in places like this."

Rachel knocked on the battered front door, which quivered to the touch. "Let's keep it simple. Remember why we're here," she said.

A woman in her fifties opened the door an inch or two and peered through the gap. She looked scared stiff. "You're police. Someone complain about the noise, did they?"

"DCI King and DS Pryce, East Manchester Serious Crime," Rachel said. "We're not here because of any complaint, Mrs . . ?"

"Jane Wignall, and it's Ms. I never married. If it's not about that pig of a landlord shouting the odds at all hours of the day and night, what is it then?"

"We're here about your brother, Joseph," Elwyn said.

"Got himself locked up again, has he? Stupid sod. He spends his life behind bars. Mind you, it's probably better than that dump he rents. At least he's warm and well fed in there. His bloody water heater's bust and the gas has been disconnected for safety reasons. He won't be saddled with those problems inside."

"Rogue landlord?" Elwyn asked.

Jane Wignall nodded. "A bloody fortune he charges too. But neither Joe or I can go anywhere else. Bad credit history."

This was all very well, but they still had to tell her what had happened to her brother. "Can we come in, Jane?" Rachel asked. "We need a private word."

"Place is a pigsty, but if you're not fussy, step inside."

The two detectives followed her through a narrow hallway and into the sitting room. She wasn't joking, the house was a mess. There were damp patches on the ceiling and the paper was peeling from the walls. Dirty crockery covered every surface, and the dust was inches thick. Some sort of insect — a cockroach? — scuttled away as Rachel walked in.

"The landlord is a tight git. I've been onto the council but they reckon it's got nowt to do with them. Mind you, they'll have to do something soon. This entire row is set for demolition within the month."

"I'm afraid we've got some bad news," Rachel began. "I'm very sorry to have to tell you, but Joseph is dead."

Jane Wignall turned pale. "I knew he were bad with his heart, but dead! When did this happen?"

"It wasn't his heart, Jane. Joseph was murdered. He was living in a nursing home in Ancoats under the name of Francis Baslow. We think it was Baslow the killer was after, and not Joseph." Rachel gave her a minute to take this in, she looked dazed. "Does that name mean anything to you?"

Jane shook her head. "I don't understand. I've never heard of this man, and what was Joe doing in a nursing home? There's no way he could have afforded the fees them places charge."

"When did you last see Joseph?" Elwyn asked.

"I'm not sure. His lad rang me and said he were in hospital. I meant to visit, but it meant dragging all the way out to Wythenshawe and the bus fare's a killer. It was either pay that or eat."

"He was friendly with another man in there, the Francis Baslow I mentioned. Did Joseph's son mention him?"

"No. All he told me was that Joe were bad. He didn't suffer, did he?"

"No, Jane, he was suffocated while he slept. I doubt he'd have known anything about it. He was very ill and on a lot of medication."

"That's something, at least. It could have been worse. Joe mixed with the wrong crowd, even as a kid. I tried with him, I really did. He was interested in photography and he was good too — wildlife mostly. I encouraged him to enter a couple of competitions but he was too busy with other stuff. Lately, he'd got himself involved with a right rogue. He owed him money and was scared stiff."

"Do you have a name for this man?" Rachel asked.

"No. Joe never told me. The man had money, I know that much. He gave Joe a small fortune up front for a job he wanted him to do. He came round here once, to pick Joe up. You should have seen the car he drove. A shiny black sports job it was. Joe needed the work and seemed dead happy about it — thought he'd finally fallen on his feet. But that was before he knew what the work was."

A wealthy man in a fancy car, it could have been anyone. But the Blakes had owned a black sports job. Rachel had seen it parked outside that club of theirs on the morning they'd rescued Jonny, after his run-in with Danulescu. "Are you sure you can't recall the man's name?" Rachel asked.

"He never said. I always thought it best to keep my nose out of Joe's business."

"What did the bloke want him to do?" asked Elwyn.

"It were a driving job. Before he left, he told me he wished he hadn't agreed to it, but once he'd taken the money, it was too late to back out." She looked at Rachel, no doubt considering what to say next without incriminating herself. "Joe was a long-distance lorry driver. Not that he'd done much of that recently, but he still had his license."

"Your brother drove for this man? Did he run a haulage firm?" Rachel asked.

"No. All I know about him is that he is wealthy. Joe said he owns a lot of property around Manchester. The smart end, not rat-infested places like this. He rents it out."

That was a fair description of Jed McAteer.

"This bloke wanted Joe to travel across Europe with an empty container and bring stuff back. Joe didn't think much about it, it sounded like a standard enough job. But it wasn't that simple."

"What do you mean?" Elwyn asked.

"When he got back after the first trip, he came round 'ere in a right state. He was really upset. He was ill too, with his heart. The stress had made his condition worse. Joe said he'd been tricked and that the man had gone too far."

"Was it drugs?"

Jane Wignall looked Rachel in the eyes and shook her head. "No. That Joe could have coped with, he wasn't no angel." She hesitated for a few moments. "It was people."

Rachel's stomach formed a knot. The link with the trafficking case had just got stronger. "You're sure? He couldn't have been mistaken?"

"They were crowded into that container — teenage girls mostly."

Ronan and Leonora Blake had been trafficking girls from Eastern Europe. A number of them had worked in their clubs around Manchester. Jane Wignall's story fitted.

"He only did the one trip. By the time they reached Manchester, one of the girls was dead. Joe was terrified. He never did find out what happened to the body. He didn't know what to do. The man he worked for didn't seem bothered, said to forget about it. When Joe said he was doing no more runs, things got ugly. They beat him up. He had a heart attack and ended up in hospital. I rang him a couple of times and tried to get him to come clean. He was terrified of the police finding out, and even more of the man who'd hired him. I've heard nothing from him since he was discharged."

"If it's any consolation, his murder had nothing to do with the people trafficking, Jane. Those people didn't find him," Rachel said. "Joe's death was down to something else entirely. We think he took the identity of a man he befriended in hospital. For the last three months he was living in a nursing home, posing as this man."

"I had no idea," Jane Wignall said. "Most of the time I thought he was dead, killed by that villain. If I'd of known, I would have gone to see him." Jane Wignall took a set of keys off a table and handed them to Rachel. "He lived up the road. Number sixteen. I've been in a couple of times to make sure the place hasn't been done over, but it's fine — well, in no worse a state than when he lived there. There is something else, though. When he was working for this bloke, he was terrified like I said. Joe told me he'd got himself some insurance, and that if anything went wrong, I should use it."

"Do you know what that insurance was?" Rachel asked.

"I've no idea. He wouldn't say, just that it were in the house."

"Thank you. Do you know where I can find Joseph's son?"

"He doesn't live local anymore. He moved down south over a year ago, and I haven't heard from him since. This is the number he used to have, but I can't get anywhere with it." She scribbled the number on a scrap of paper and handed it to Rachel.

Rachel thanked her. "I'll get a colleague to take you to identify Joe later today."

CHAPTER NINE

Back in the car, Rachel rang Jude and gave her Joseph Wignall's address. "The house needs sweeping for prints and DNA. You never know, we might get lucky. Wignall was being pressurised by a local villain. I need to know who that was. Would you check for Baslow's prints and DNA too? He had to have gone somewhere when he left the hospital. Elwyn and I will have a look around too. Wignall had supposedly hidden something there, although we've no idea what it is. Anything odd you find, Jude, let us know."

"We'll get on it. I'll be in touch."

"From the description his sister gave us, I think we can guess who the villain was, don't you, Rachel?" Elwyn said. "She gave a pretty good description of McAteer."

"A villain with property. That could be anyone, and you know it. I've told you, Elwyn, Jed would never get involved in people trafficking."

"And when Jude comes up with McAteer's prints in that house? What then?"

"She won't." Rachel was well aware that Elwyn thought she wrong to stick up for McAteer, but she knew him. He was a villain, sure, but he would never sell another human being to make money.

"We have no names and no proof, just hearsay from a grieving sister. We do nothing for now," Rachel said.

"And what about Kenton? The trafficking case is his. The merest whiff of Wignall's involvement and he'll be all over it like a rash. Wignall's name could well have come up during the investigation. You haven't seen the file so you can't be sure. You have to tell him what you've discovered. He'll not appreciate being kept in the dark." Elwyn started the engine. "Where to? Up the street to Wignall's place?"

Rachel suddenly remembered that she'd left Wignall's name emblazoned across the incident board. Things had changed. If Elwyn thought that Jane Wignall's evidence added up to McAteer, then Kenton was bound to jump to the same conclusion. Elwyn was right. If Kenton recognised Wignall's name, he'd want in and that would mean trouble. She had to remove it from the board before he arrived to pick her up later.

"There's something at the station I need to do. We'll go there first and then come back and look at Wignall's house. And you can forget about McAteer being involved. The case we're working on involves the murder of two people, Wignall and Longhurst. The killer thought Wignall was Baslow, I'd stake my career on it. That's the reason we're looking at Wignall's life. We need to know if Baslow got mixed up in something he couldn't handle." That was Rachel's official stance. Privately, she'd make her own enquiries, and that wasn't up for discussion, not even with Elwyn.

"Meanwhile, we might have stumbled on the proof Kenton needs to arrest McAteer, but you don't want to use it." Elwyn sounded exasperated.

"It's not proof, far from it. Leave it, Elwyn. Let Kenton do his own investigating. McAteer will surface soon enough. In any case, Kenton will no doubt have an international warrant out for his arrest. I just hope he's keeping his head down."

"Short-sighted, Rachel. Not your best idea."

Elwyn drove them back to the station while Rachel sat wrestling with her conscience. What if Elwyn was right and

Jed was behind the trafficking? As much as she doubted it, she couldn't refute the evidence, mainly that he'd done a runner. This wasn't something he'd ever done before. Then there was the file of evidence Kenton reckoned he'd gathered against him, not that he'd produced it. Apart from the Blakes, she had no idea what circles Jed moved in these days. On the surface, he appeared to be a successful property developer but was that the truth of the matter? Had he got himself into a financial mess and was he using this as his way out?

* * *

Back in the incident room, Jonny and Amy were busy researching their two victims.

"Woodsmoor Investments Ltd, ma'am. I have more information about them," Amy told Rachel. "They sold retirement homes in deepest Cheshire. The company owned a plot of land and had plans drawn up for a hundred bungalows to be built. It was marketed as an entire community, the perfect place to retire to. There was to be a fishing lake, a restaurant and other facilities."

"Sounds wonderful, so what happened?"

"Nothing. The properties were never built. The company had a glossy brochure produced and there was a huge advertising campaign. A lot of people bought in. The bungalows sold at a reasonable price, but a hefty deposit was needed to secure a plot."

"Have you found anyone who can enlighten us as to what went on? Why it went down the pan?" Rachel asked.

"No, ma'am. So far, my research has only come up with the three names — Baslow, Longhurst and Graham. Longhurst dealt with the customers and Baslow worked in the background. What Graham's role was, I'm not sure."

"Baslow was a silent partner. Perhaps he put up the money. But we'll get nothing from either of them, not unless Baslow turns up, that is. Any ideas?" Rachel said.

"No, but Alison Longhurst's sister has asked to see you, ma'am," Amy said. "I've left her address and number on your desk."

"Thanks, Amy, and good work. It would be handy to see a copy of that brochure. Once we find an ex-customer, we'll ask them."

"The super's stand-in has arrived," Jonny announced. "He hasn't shown his face yet, the desk sergeant showed him into Harding's office and gave us the nod."

Just what she needed. "Did the sergeant say who he is?"

"No, ma'am."

Rachel took a deep breath and made her way to Harding's office. Hopefully, the new incumbent wasn't some idiot who'd need carrying. What the team needed was to be left alone to get on with the job. Rachel tapped on the door and walked in. Her blood froze.

Mark Kenton was sitting at Harding's desk. She might have known. Kenton was a career copper, determined to get on and climb the ladder, no matter what. Harding was seriously ill, he might not return. Heaven help them if this became a permanent arrangement.

"I saw you the other night. You didn't say anything about this then," Rachel said.

"Drop the attitude, Rachel, it doesn't do you any favours. Why not wish me well and leave it at that?"

"You should have told me."

"I didn't know myself then. Sit down. We need to have a chat."

There was a smile on his lips but it didn't reach the eyes. This was Kenton doing what he did best, lording it over his colleagues. "You're here, the acting super, in charge, what else is there to say?" she said.

"You can start by bringing me up to speed with your current investigation," Kenton said.

"We have two victims so far. They were partners in a leisure start-up business. They convinced people to part with their hard-earned cash, knowing it was doubtful they'd get anything in return. We're looking for someone they upset as their potential killer. For reasons we don't understand, both victims' ring fingers were taken as trophies and confetti was left at the crime scenes."

"Any complications?" he asked.

Rachel shook her head. "There's a third possible victim we still have to find, but we're going down the usual route — background and families."

Rachel saw his expression soften. "Good, you seem to have things under control. Anything tricky turns up, let me know at once."

"Is that all?" She hesitated. "Harding said that you had the Blake file. Can I have a look at it?"

"Sorry, Rachel, no, you can't. I haven't got it with me."

Rachel could see the file on top of a pile of others on his desk. Her eyes were immediately drawn to a file bound in red that had the name 'Blake' written on it. She leaned forward and grabbed it. "This looks like it to me. Why lie, Mark?"

"Give it here, Rachel." Avoiding her eyes, Kenton held out his hand. "That file is confidential and the case is still open."

He sounded wary. What was wrong? Her gaze fell on the cover again. The name Blake had been handwritten beneath the title, 'Operation GoldStar.' It rang a vague bell. The GoldStar case was a couple of years old and involved a number of murders in Manchester, which were thought to be the work of an organised crime gang. Although she wouldn't put anything past Ronan Blake, she'd been under the impression that he was purely trafficking, and as far as she knew, he hadn't killed anyone. He was motivated by money, pure and simple.

"What has 'Operation GoldStar' got to do with the Blake case?" she asked. "Are the two linked?"

"Nothing to do with that file or GoldStar has anything to do with you. Just give the file back and forget it."

Reluctantly, she handed it over. "Okay, but I can still read what's on the system."

"You'll be disappointed. The operation doesn't exist. You haven't seen the file or what's written on it." He tapped the cover.

"Does Harding know about this?" she asked.

"I doubt it. Speaking of Harding, his filing system has no logic to it."

"What are you looking for?" Rachel asked. "Perhaps you'll find what you need among that lot on his desk. Don't be too critical of Harding. He's had a lot on his plate. He's been ill."

"He's very ill, Rachel. He should have stopped working weeks ago. This is what happens when people don't listen to the voice of reason."

"Yes, but as a rule Harding is highly organised. I'm sure that whatever you want will turn up."

"Keep me up to date. Any arrests, let me know." She was dismissed.

Rachel hesitated by the door. "How does your new position impact on our dinner?"

"It doesn't," he said. "We're merely meeting to discuss your caseload."

"We could do that here."

"Don't make it complicated, Rachel. Simply keep the dinner between ourselves."

Rachel returned to the incident room just in time to take a call from Jude.

"The PMs will be done at four this afternoon," Jude said. "Alison Longhurst's sister has identified the body, and Wignall's has been here too."

"Me and Elwyn will be there." Rachel put the phone down.

"How is he, our new leader?" Elwyn asked.

"Gunning for the old one. Not that I'm surprised. They've given us Kenton." Rachel waited for Elwyn's reaction but it never came.

"I half expected it," he said. "My advice, for what it's worth, is either tell him what you know or go extra careful."

Rachel pulled a face. "I still can't decide what to do. I can't work out what he's up to. Have you heard of Operation GoldStar? Kenton has a file with that title. I grabbed hold of it, and he looked terrified. He obviously didn't want me seeing whatever little gems it contained."

Elwyn shook his head. "All I know is, that case was poison. Don't get involved, Rachel. Do what Kenton says and drop it. There was what amounted to gang warfare on the Manchester streets at the time. In the end, some big crime boss won the day and we've been looking for him ever since."

"Which big crime boss?"

"That, Rachel, is the million-dollar question. We've no idea who he is and no one is talking."

"Kenton reckons Harding didn't know about the operation," she said.

Elwyn shrugged. "Possible, but that depends if it crossed our patch."

Rachel was uneasy. She had a horrible feeling that Kenton might have Jed in the frame. "I want Kenton gone, Elwyn. He's going to stir up trouble, I know it. He's already criticising Harding's filing system. I bet a whole lot of stuff gets blamed on the super while he's gone. It isn't fair. Harding's not here to stick up for himself."

"It's simple, Rachel. Kenton wants his job. He's younger, more ambitious and gets results. He paints the sick and ageing Harding as no longer up to it and he's halfway there. We'll just have to do what we can to watch his back while he's gone."

CHAPTER TEN

Pulling up outside Joseph Wignall's house, on the same street as his sister's place, Rachel pointed out a window on the ground floor. "It's open. Look, that net curtain is blowing about in the wind."

They got out of the car. "The frame will have warped. The thing probably won't close," Emlyn said. "You've seen the signs, these are coming down any day now, so no one's going to take an interest in a break-in."

"That window looks as if someone has prised it open and gone inside. We need to know who that was, and if they're connected to the case and not just dossing down for the night."

The detectives put on nitrile gloves. "I'll get Jude to go over it for prints. Come on then, let's see what we've got," Rachel said.

The interior of the house mirrored the outside. There'd been nothing done to it in years. Not only that, it was filthy. All sorts of stuff was piled high in the corners of the sitting room — mostly papers, boxes, and black rubbish bags.

"Untidy sod, wasn't he?" Elwyn said. "Shame though, the place has possibilities. Look at that fireplace. I reckon it's original."

Rachel gave it a glance. "There are photos everywhere. Look at these on the mantelpiece. Some of them are pretty good." She picked up a couple and examined them. "Gather them up and we'll give them a look-over back at the station. They might give us an insight into his life."

Elwyn spent the next few minutes carefully packing several dozen photos and their frames into evidence bags.

"I'll take a look upstairs," Rachel said. The place was still and quiet. The absence of noise from neighbours or traffic outside gave the house a weird atmosphere, as if it was hiding something. Rachel shuddered. The last time she'd been in a house that felt like this, she'd found a dead body screwed to a chair. The memory sent shivers down her spine. Time to get out.

"Someone's been sleeping down here," Elwyn shouted up to her.

Rachel took a last look around but there was nothing upstairs. Both bedrooms were empty, neither of them even had a bed. She went back down to join Elwyn.

"Look what I found stashed under that table. It's a sleeping bag. There's a flask and several empty sandwich cartons, recently discarded from the look of them."

"D'you think we disturbed someone, Elwyn? A homeless person perhaps. Maybe he took one look at the pair of us and did one."

"It's more likely to have been someone closer to home. Could be Baslow," Elwyn said.

"Do these houses have cellars?" Rachel asked.

"I can't see a door. No, I reckon this is all you get."

"I want to know who the landlord is," Rachel said. "These properties are the pits. Making people pay rent for places like this, it shouldn't be allowed."

Elwyn looked unhappy. "It isn't any of our business, Rachel. As you said, Wignall was murdered because they thought he was Baslow. It should be Kenton investigating any evidence this house might hold. You have to watch your step. Have you forgotten that Wignall's name has been linked with that of Danulescu, and so by default to the trafficking case?"

Rachel was tired of hearing the same old warning. "Give me a break, Elwyn. There's no harm in giving the place a look. We need it checking over by scenes-of-crime anyway. Baslow might have come here, remember."

"Rachel, you need to stop this and tell Kenton what you know. You should hand this part of the case over without delay."

Rachel flashed him an angry glance. "Just you remember who the senior investigating officer is! Wignall *is* part of our case, Elwyn. Before I tell Kenton what we know, I want to be sure of the facts."

Elwyn shook his head. He didn't buy that one for a second. "You want to be sure McAteer won't be implicated, you mean."

Rachel groaned. She shouldn't have barked at Elwyn. It wasn't fair. He was right. "Sorry, it's not your fault. I'm a bad-tempered bitch, I know. You and the team deserve medals for putting up with me. But, please, just bear with me for a little longer."

"Not often I get an apology from you," Elwyn said. "What's up?"

"This whole bloody case, that's what. I'm terrified, Elwyn. What if Jed *is* involved in this sorry mess? He's Mia's father for heaven's sake. What will it do to her if she finds out?"

"You need to stop over-thinking it. Mia will be fine. You also need to rein it in. Biting off everyone's head, going around like the wicked witch of the west won't get you anywhere except number one in the unpopularity stakes."

"You're right, and I don't want that," Rachel said. "I don't need everyone to like me but I do need their cooperation."

"Then take my advice. Pass this little lot on to Kenton and take a step back."

"We need to get Jude and her team round here. With luck she'll find out who's been sleeping here, and what other information it holds. I want the truth, Elwyn, every bit as much as you do. If this house reveals McAteer's prints, then I'll be first in line to bring him to justice."

"Speaking of Jude, we should be leaving for the PMs," Elwyn said.

Rachel nodded. "You can drive."

* * *

It wasn't far into central Manchester and the facility where Jude and Butterworth were based.

Butterworth seemed to be on his own. He nodded at the body of Joseph Wignall laid out on the table. "Him first."

"Is Jude here?" Rachel asked.

"Dr Glover has been called away. Such is her reputation these days that the Staffordshire force have asked to borrow her."

"But she will be back?"

"Oh yes. Later today."

Rachel looked down at Wignall's emaciated body. What had happened between him and Baslow? Had they both agreed to the identity swap, or had Baslow been coerced? If he was still alive, they needed to find him.

"His heart was shot. The mitral valve is badly diseased and the coronary arteries are furred up. Bypass surgery and valve replacement might have given him longer, but he was unlikely to have survived such an operation, given his general condition."

"Poor bloke. Any idea how he got so bad?" Elwyn asked.

"His lungs indicate that he was a heavy smoker. We have tested for drugs and found opiates, and not from any pain medication he may have been taking. He may have been in a nursing home, but he was getting a regular supply. Look at his lower legs — see the track marks?"

Another word with Pat Wentworth was needed.

"He had to have had help, Elwyn, someone to bring it in for him. That would have required cash too. His sister said she checked his bank account, so where did it come from?"

"Perhaps the same person who passed on the entry key code to whoever murdered him," Elwyn said.

"We found fibres from the pillow in his mouth," Butterworth confirmed. "He died as a result of suffocation."

Butterfield removed his mask and changed his gown, ready for the next one. The three of them and the technician moved into the adjoining room, where Alison Longhurst lay on the table, covered by a white sheet.

"There's a nasty bump on the back of her head. We extracted some fragments of rust, so something metal was used to hit her. We found blue fibres in her mouth but not from a pillow. The fibres were long, and synthetic."

"Like a sofa cushion?" Elwyn asked.

"Possibly, but according to Dr Glover there was nothing like that in the house."

Rachel nodded. "He brought it with him. He knew exactly what he was going to do, and came prepared."

"I've had a look at her GP's notes. She was a healthy woman. There is nothing remarkable about the body otherwise."

CHAPTER ELEVEN

"We'll speak to Pat Wentworth on the way back to the station," Rachel said. "We need to interview the staff as soon as possible, it's now a matter of urgency. One of them is supplying drugs. Did you see Wignall's lower legs? There were track marks alright but no infection. Those injections were given by someone who knew the ropes, using clean needles."

"What about the vicar?" Elwyn said. "He visited regularly. He'd have access to money, but then where would he get the heroin from? He's a churchman, it's unlikely he's the dealer."

"You and I both know that all kinds of people become dealers for all sorts of reasons," Rachel said.

Elwyn was right. It was time they questioned him.

"What's the chance that Sankey paid the dealer and got one of the nurses to administer the heroin? Perhaps he paid her too."

"We'll visit both the vicar and Hawthorne Lodge, and then we'll call it a day. Whatever happened, it doesn't put that home in a good light, does it, Elwyn? Pat Wentworth has a lot to lose by not helping us," Rachel said. "I was hoping the post-mortems would throw up more than they did. We're still none the wiser about why our victims had to die."

"One thing we do know, Rachel. Whoever did it, didn't know Baslow very well. Otherwise they would have realised that it was the wrong man."

A good point. Rachel was about to discuss it further when her mobile beeped with a text message. She read it through and then exclaimed, "Shona! I'd forgotten all about her."

"Go on, tell us. What's happened now?"

"Shona, an old friend of mine from uni, is getting married. She's been living with her boyfriend Juan for ages and they've finally decided to make it legal. She asked me to be a bridesmaid, weeks ago, but I've been so busy I didn't realise how close it was getting to the big day."

"You've not mentioned her before," Elwyn said.

"I don't see or hear from her much, that's why. Shona lives in Spain, near Malaga. She went out there to work about ten years ago, met Juan and never came back. We were best buddies at uni, shared a flat, clothes, told each other everything. Back then we were really close, but given the distance between us, I've rarely seen her since. We just do Christmas cards and birthdays and have spoken a few times over the phone. She's the only friend from those days that I've kept in touch with."

"Not quite, Rachel. Don't forget McAteer. Did Shona know him?"

"Yes. Shona, me, Jed and a lad called Liam used to pal around together. She's really keen on me being a bridesmaid at her wedding." She turned to Elwyn, smiling. "I can't see me in yards of peach tulle, can you?"

"When is it happening?"

"Four days from now, plenty of notice — not! She might have told me earlier, she knows how I'm fixed."

"She did tell you earlier, so perhaps you should have told her definitely one way or another. Will you go?"

"I never know how busy I'm going to be, and I don't see how I can now. We're in the middle of this case, and there's the kids to sort."

"Alan will see to the girls, as well you know, and we might have cracked this case by next week. If I were you, I'd get my flight booked."

"I'll think about it. If I change my mind, I'll do it online. But realistically, how can I go? We've got two bodies and no motive as yet. Anyway, I can't leave my precious team in Kenton's hands. He'll have you all climbing the walls."

"Precious, are we? Not the impression I get."

"Get over yourself, Elwyn. You know how well we all work together."

Elwyn pulled up outside Saint Paul's vicarage. "Can I suggest we treat this delicately? The good vicar might not have anything to do with it at all."

"We'll see how he reacts first."

The man who answered the door was small and overweight. Bald, with a round, red face.

He beamed, apparently unsurprised to see them. "You look like police officers to me. This will be about poor Francis I expect. Come inside." They followed him into a sitting room furnished as if for a meeting, cluttered with chairs and small side tables.

"Just a few questions, to clear up one or two details," Rachel said, taking one of the chairs at random. "You appear to be the only visitor Francis ever had. Were you aware of that?"

"Mrs Wentworth told me. I did wonder why the daughter never came, but I presumed she had her reasons. Francis didn't speak about her much, or his son. Towards the end, he was too weak for conversation anyway."

"You may not be aware of this, but the man who was killed in Hawthorne Lodge wasn't Francis Baslow. At some point Francis had swapped places with a man called Joseph Wignall. Did he speak to you about this?" asked Rachel

The vicar gaped at her. "No, I had no idea. Not that it would have made any difference. No matter who he was, he was a man in torment and needed my help."

"In what way was he in torment?" Elwyn asked.

"He was troubled, afraid. I offered my help but he wouldn't confide in me. If he had, I would have done my best for him. I got the impression he feared for his life. When I learned he'd been murdered, it didn't come as much of a surprise."

"And you didn't report it?" asked Elwyn.

"It was simply a feeling, nothing tangible. Even if I'd asked, Francis wouldn't have said anything."

"Joseph, not Francis," Rachel said. "We've just come from Joseph Wignall's post-mortem." She saw no point in going round the houses. "He was a regular heroin user and could not possibly have got the stuff for himself. You, Reverend, were his only visitor."

He stared at them both for a few seconds. "Whatever he took, I can assure you it had nothing to do with me. Where on earth do you imagine I'd get heroin from? I wouldn't know where to start."

"Have you ever met Julia Baslow?" Rachel asked.

"No, never. Is that important?"

"I'm trying to discover how a sick man in a nursing home gets hold of the money he'd need to pay for his fix. Julia had control of the purse strings. She could have paid someone to sort it for her father."

"What is this? Some lonely old man dies in a nursing home, and suddenly, his daughter and I are drug dealers. I've never heard such nonsense." He stood up. "If the man who died wasn't Francis, I take it you're looking for him."

"We're doing the best we can," Rachel said. "But we've no idea where he might have gone."

"Can I suggest that you speak to the home again?" Sankey said. "See if they can offer an explanation."

"Oh, we intend to, but I wanted you to have the opportunity to tell us what you know first."

The vicar regarded Rachel sternly. "I want you to go now, and if you wish to come again, kindly make an appointment. I've told you everything I can."

Back in the car, Elwyn said, "He made that plain enough. Perhaps he has a point, Rachel. We do keep throwing things at Julia — and now him."

Rachel ignored the jibe. "Pat Wentworth next and then back to the station." She checked her watch. "I'm supposed to be having dinner with Kenton, but I will have to cry off."

"He won't like that."

"He'll have to lump it. The man's just playing games anyway."

* * *

Pat Wentworth was outraged at the accusation. "Heroin? Where would he get that from?"

"We were hoping you could tell us," Rachel said. "He was a regular user, so someone here must have supplied him."

"No one here would do such a thing. All of my staff are checked by the CRB, and they're all trustworthy."

"Not quite. There's still the question of how the killer got hold of the entry code. Someone must have given it to him. Joseph Wignall, the man you knew as Francis Baslow, was supplied with heroin, probably paid cash and was given help to inject it. There are track marks on his lower legs and no sign of infection. How do you explain that?"

Pat Wentworth looked confused. "Well, I can't. And as far as I'm aware, he had no cash. He didn't need it. We supply everything, including the daily papers. He couldn't go out and had no visitors other than the vicar."

"We've spoken to his sister and the vicar, and they insist it must be down to someone here," Elwyn said.

"It sounds improbable, but they have to be lying."

"Mrs Wentworth, we intend to return in the morning and interview every member of your staff. We'll also speak to any of the residents who are up to answering our questions."

CHAPTER TWELVE

Day Four

"You haven't said a word to me in days," Mia said at breakfast the next morning. "I ask a simple question and you go off on one."

"Don't be ridiculous, Mia. I've been busy, that's all. I've been leaving for work long before you are even out of bed, and you slept at Ella's last night." Rachel nodded at the mobile in her daughter's hand. "What am I supposed to do, ring you on that?"

"A simple yes or no will do: is he or isn't he?" Mia said. "Ella reckons your behaviour is suspicious and that you must have something to hide."

This required a firm, no nonsense reply. "Both you and Ella are totally wrong. Alan is your dad. Anyway, how could it be Jed? My romance with him finished when I was Meggy's age, so how did we conceive you?"

"I'm not stupid, Mum. You'll have met up since."

Mia was far too close to the truth for comfort. "Don't be daft. When would I get the time for a start? All my holiday entitlement is taken up by you two."

"Well, there's something," Mia said. "And don't think I'm going to give up. I'll ask Jed when he surfaces again. He'll tell me the truth."

"Right. School. Get your stuff or you'll miss the bus."

Rachel picked up a slice of toast and wandered into the sitting room. A late start was all very well but she could have done without the third degree from her youngest. Picking up her mobile off the coffee table, she rang Elwyn at the station.

"We'll have a word with Alison Longhurst's sister this morning, see what she can throw into the pot. How are Jonny and Amy doing?"

"Jonny has been at the hospital all night with his dad. He took a turn for the worse, and Amy hasn't turned up."

Rachel was surprised about Amy. "That's not like her. Do we know anything?"

"No, Rachel, she seemed fine yesterday — a little quiet recently perhaps, but she's had her head down."

Elwyn was right, she had been quiet, working hard too. That was unusual for Amy, the flakiest member of the team. "Give her a ring and get back to me. As for Jonny, we'll give him some space. He'll be back when he's ready."

"I'll meet you at Beattie Reilly's," Elwyn said.

"Call her first, so she knows we're coming."

* * *

DC Amy Metcalfe hadn't taken time off in a while so she didn't feel too guilty about today. Besides, it was an emergency. She rang in early and told the desk sergeant she'd been throwing up all night, and to let DCI King know. She cracked a half-hearted joke about canteen food and left it at that.

Work sorted, she checked her mobile, biting her bottom lip as she scanned through the missed messages — eight of them, all left by Connor Young, and each more threatening than the last. Her hands shaking, she tapped in a response.

Yes, she'd meet him, but not round here. She knew a beauty spot a few miles out of the city that would be perfect, a reservoir popular with walkers spending a weekend in the Pennines. On a weekday it would be deserted and anyway, no one would recognise her up there.

Amy knew that it was stupid to agree to meet him, but what choice did she have? Connor Young had to be stopped. He'd got his claws into her brother, Aiden, and wouldn't let go. Aiden Metcalfe was an addict and relied on the thug for drugs. If that wasn't bad enough, Connor had found out that she too occasionally bought heroin for Aiden. The job had a lot of drawbacks, but it did mean she knew her fair share of rogues.

Amy had formulated a plan of sorts. She'd threaten Connor, tell him that she knew people every bit as bad as the ones he did. One word in the right ear and he'd disappear forever. She tried to convince herself that it would work, but she knew she was kidding herself. All Connor had to do was shoot his mouth off, tell the wrong person, and her career would be toast.

The messages were a new thing. Aiden must have run up a shed load of debt for Connor to pile on the pressure like this. She'd try the reasonable approach first, promise to straighten up as soon as she could. If that didn't satisfy the little scrote, she'd resort to the threats. It was a game of bluff. All she had to do was hold her nerve.

As she drove towards Ashton, she considered the consequences of her actions. If she found out, DCI King would finish her. It would be career over. Amy slapped her hands on the steering wheel. Why did this have to happen to her? Aiden, her lazy, feckless, addict of a brother had got her into this, begging her to help him get a bunch of thugs off his back. What was she supposed to do? Let the likes of Connor Young and his cronies beat him to a pulp? She felt like screaming.

At Ashton, Amy carried on towards Stalybridge and took the road to Greenfield. She drove through the village and then joined the narrow road that led up to the reservoir in the hills. Mid-week, the place was deserted. Return at the weekend and it'd be like a holiday resort, with walkers and climbers making their way up into the hills surrounding the huge expanse of water.

Amy pulled into the small parking area and looked around. Connor Young was waiting for her. She spotted his old Ford under some trees. She shuddered. Aiden was a slightly built lad, Young was tall and thickset. If he set about her brother, he'd kill him.

"Before you start, I've no money for you," Amy shouted. "So your stupid threats won't work."

He leant against his car, grinning at her. "Feisty piece of work, aren't you? What makes you think this is about money?"

Amy walked towards him. "Isn't it always? My brother's an idiot, but I won't see him harmed by the likes of you. I'll get you sorted myself first, and don't think I can't. The job I've got, I meet the right sort of people."

"No you won't, missy. You'll do as you're told. Anyway, it's not money I'm after."

That threw her. If not money, then what? "Go on then, surprise me."

"I want you to get something for me."

"What?"

"You found a dead 'un the other night in one of them old folks' homes. Who was he?"

"What's it to you?"

Connor Young grabbed Amy by the lapel of her jacket. "If you want to keep those pretty looks, you'll talk to me. His name, missy."

"Joseph Wignall," she said. "It's no secret. Why are you so interested?"

"He's got something of mine."

Amy was curious. What could possibly link Wignall to this piece of rubbish? Then she remembered. Wignall was an addict too. DCI King had put that very fact on the incident board only yesterday.

"And you want this something back?"

He smirked. "Easy to see why you're a detective."

"It won't be possible. Anything taken from that room will be securely locked in our evidence store. If it wasn't, it'll still be in the house and there'll be a PC watching that."

"You'll find a way. No one will miss what I want. Get it and Aiden's debts will be wiped."

It was certainly appealing. Amy didn't know how much her brother owed, but it might run to thousands. "Get what?"

"A simple little photograph." He smiled at her. "Nothing too complicated, is it? Your lot will have found dozens in that house, so you'll have to have a good look through them. I want the want the one of three men taken in front of the Midland Hotel in Manchester. There's just the one, so you can't miss it. Get the photo, text me and we'll meet up again."

CHAPTER THIRTEEN

Beatrice Reilly, known as Beattie, lived a couple of miles away from her sister, Alison Longhurst, in a large house with a huge front garden. Tucked to one side of the drive was an old camper van.

Rachel reckoned there was only a couple of years between them, although Beattie looked nothing like her sister. The woman in the morgue was blonde, whereas Beattie had black hair cropped very short. She was bigger built too.

"I lived close by in case Alison needed help with the boys. She was a single parent and I have no children. I even changed my pattern of work so that I could help, but Alison didn't appreciate it. She called it 'interference,' and we argued," Beattie said.

"What about Alison's husband? Doesn't he help with the boys?"

Beattie pulled a face. "The man's a total waste of space. He left them years ago, never made contact and never provided a penny for those boys. He took off with another woman, went to live abroad somewhere and left Alison to it. That's why she had to work so hard. It was down to her to put a roof over their heads and food on the table."

"Do you know where he is now? However badly he behaved, we should tell him what's happened."

"I have no idea. One of the boys might know, I suppose. Once he left, Alison never spoke about him again."

Rachel regarded the tearful Beattie Reilly. She sat on the sofa, with Len Partington in close attendance. She wasn't shamming, she was genuinely upset about losing her sister.

"At some stage, I or one of my officers will have to speak to the boys, particularly the one who found his mum. It would help if you were present. Perhaps you could prepare the way for me."

"Yes, okay. They're putting on a brave face, but don't put any pressure on," Beattie said.

"You two live here together?" Rachel asked.

Beattie looked round at Len and smiled. "On and off. The flat he lives in needs extensive repairs and the landlord was taking his time, so I said he could come here."

"How long have you been together?" Elwyn asked.

"Only a few weeks." She patted his hand. "But you know, don't you? This time it's for keeps, isn't it, Len?"

Len nodded, putting a protective arm around her shoulder. "We're determined to make a go of it."

"Is that your caravan outside?" Rachel asked.

"Yes. Before I moved into the house, Beattie let me park it up on the drive. It worked for a while, but it's not much fun at this time of year."

"Did you know Alison?" Rachel asked him.

"Not really. We didn't have time to know each other properly. We spoke on the phone though. My interaction with Alison consisted mostly of relaying messages between her and Beattie."

"But you did meet her?" Rachel said.

Beattie shook her head and looked away. "Alison could be difficult. She didn't want my help but that didn't stop her going on about how my relationship with Len would change things. I think she was terrified I would move away and she'd be left alone. Len and me, we'd talked about living by the coast, you see, just idle chat but that did it, Alison refused to have anything to do with him. I know she wanted me to end it, for things to go back to the way they were before I met Len." Beattie took hold of his hand. "But she had no reason to worry. I knew how she felt, and we would never have left her alone."

"How was Alison in general recently? Did she mention anyone worrying her? Was she more edgy than usual?" Rachel asked.

Beattie shook her head. "No, Alison was fine. If someone had been bothering her, I'm sure she would have told me. She wasn't afraid of much, and she'd had some tough times in the past."

"We know she had several failed businesses under her belt. That must have been hard to take. Do you know if she upset anyone at those times? Perhaps a customer or a supplier?" Rachel asked.

"Businesses go bump all the time. Alison was philosophical about it. She used to say that it was only money and there were far worse things to worry about."

"Did she ever talk to you about her last business partner, Francis Baslow?"

Beattie Reilly shook her head, frowning. "Baslow? No, I don't recall the name. The last venture she was involved in was a development of country properties in Cheshire and she mostly worked with a man called Sam Graham. She put a lot of money into it. Her and Sam owned two thirds of the company between them. I knew there was a third shareholder, a silent partner. Perhaps that was this Baslow man. Alison never mentioned his name."

"Do you know where we can find Sam Graham?" Rachel asked

"If he's any sense, he'll have done one," Len Partington said.

Beattie gave him a filthy look.

He shook his head. "It's no use, Beattie, it needs saying. This Baslow was most likely the brains behind the operation.

77

To my reckoning, he was nothing but a crook, and you're glossing it over. I took a ride out there when it went down. The site was nothing but a patch of rough ground on the outskirts of Chester. There was no way retirement bungalows or anything else could be erected there, and there certainly wasn't room for a fishing lake. The truth is, the whole thing was a scam, nothing more than daylight robbery. Anyone who paid over good money lost the lot, simple as that."

"The company was set up with the best of intentions," Beattie insisted. "Alison would never knowingly swindle folk out of money, or get herself into anything shady."

"It looks as if that's exactly what she did," said Rachel. "Perhaps not intentionally, but it could be why she got herself killed."

"You're saying that someone who bought in, a customer, killed her?" asked Beattie.

"We have to consider it. Do you have one of Woodsmoor's brochures?"

"No," Beattie said. "But I did see one. The whole thing looked lovely. If it had come to pass, I'm sure the buyers would have been happy with the deal."

Len Partington shook his head.

"Here's my card," Rachel said. "If anything occurs to you, ring me."

* * *

Rachel and Elwyn sat in the car outside the Reilly house, trying to piece together what they knew. "They were scamming money out of people. Promising them a dream in return for their investment and reneging on the deal," Rachel said.

"People shouldn't be so gullible. If I was parting with that sort of money, I'd at least want to see the site and the work in progress before I committed myself," Elwyn said.

"Baslow and the others must have spun a good yarn." Rachel did a search on her phone. She was looking for Woodsmoor. "No website, no Facebook page — nothing.

It's as if the company never existed. When we get back to the station, we'll check Companies House and I'll get IT forensics on it. They might find some historical internet data."

"It's more important that we find Sam Graham before our killer does," said Elwyn. "Odd that he's not come to us, given the news."

"He's probably terrified. We'll get the team on it once we're back."

"Do we have Alison Longhurst's phone?" asked Elwyn.

"Yes, the data from that and Wignall's should be in by now."

"Talking to the pair in there got me thinking," Elwyn said. "Perhaps we're looking at this all wrong. It could be an inside job. Have you considered that Francis Baslow might be our killer, that he planned this all along? Being in a position to swap identities with Wignall happened at just the right time. He takes the man's identity, disappears and hopes that the swap won't be discovered."

"It's a bit of a leap," Rachel said, "and why risk murder? His daughter knew straight away it wasn't him when she saw the body."

"What if she'd refused and it'd been the vicar who identified him? He wouldn't know. Given the family rift, that could quite easily have happened. Possibly Baslow thought it was a risk worth taking," Elwyn said.

"Okay, but why would Baslow kill his partners?"

"I don't know, but perhaps they threatened to shop him," Elwyn said. "Perhaps Wignall threatened to upset his plans in some way. We mustn't forget Wignall's past and the people he was involved with. Baslow was stealing, pure and simple. He could have salted the money away and they found out. We need to find him, Rachel. We have no reason to believe that he's dead and if he's not, why hasn't he come forward? The story of Wignall's death has made the papers, so if Baslow's out there, he will know."

Rachel wasn't convinced. "What about the confetti, and the amputated finger? It has to mean something to the killer."

"Not necessarily. Perhaps he did it to throw us."

"I don't think so, Elwyn. The confetti was left on the bodies for a reason."

Rachel heard a beep and checked the message on her mobile. "Shona again. She wants an answer quick." She tucked the thing into her pocket. "Why is this job so damned impossible, Elwyn? How can I possibly go gadding off to Spain with this little lot on my plate?"

"Speak to Kenton and leave the donkey work to us. You won't be gone long."

Rachel wished it was that simple. Well, maybe it was. The more she thought about it, the more the idea appealed to her. "Three days tops, I reckon. What d'you think? Should I have that word?"

"Yes. Sort it, and have your break."

CHAPTER FOURTEEN

When Rachel and Elwyn arrived back at the station, they were surprised to see Jonny Farrell seated at his desk.

"I thought you were with your dad," Rachel said. "You don't have to be here. If he's in a bad way, you should be with him."

"It was a reaction to some of the medication they gave him. He's had the op now, so he should improve. The doctor reckons a couple of days and he'll be right as rain." Jonny's face was still pale and his voice trembled slightly. He was obviously worried but trying not to show it.

"Okay," she said, "it's the soft option for you. Take one of the uniforms and have a word with the residents at Hawthorne Lodge. Elwyn and I will call in later to speak to the staff. Then if you feel up to it, you can try and find the taxi driver who transferred Wignall/Baslow to the home. The firm is called Bolton's. We still don't know if Baslow was coerced, and if so, what happened to him."

Jonny smiled. "You don't have to mollycoddle me, you know. I'm still capable of working."

"I'll be the judge of that," Rachel said. "If you find out anything interesting, give me a ring. Have we heard from Amy?"

"Still ill as far as I know, although I haven't spoken to her."

Rachel helped herself to coffee from the machine and retreated to her office. The reports on the data from Wignall's mobile phone were on her desk. The search history was interesting. Wignall had been looking at flights to a number of European destinations, the last one just over a week ago. Given his condition, how did he plan to do that? As expected, there was nothing from anyone connected with Woodsmoor.

Samuel Graham was key to finding out what really went on in that business. He could also give them an insight into what Alison Longhurst thought about Baslow's scam. Had he told his colleagues what they were up to from the outset? At what point had Longhurst and Graham realised they were ripping people off?

She placed the sheets to one side and studied the phone data. Wignall both made and received few calls. The only ones they had been able to trace were to his son and sister, another two were to and from unregistered pay-as-you-go phones.

Did one of the unregistered phones belong to his supplier? The messages were puzzling, nothing more than an emoji, a smiley face winking. Some sort of code? Was this Wignall's way of telling whoever that he needed a fix? Rachel also wondered if Wignall was the only addict in Hawthorne. They needed to speak to the staff as soon as possible. She looked out into the main office, everyone was busy. Rachel accessed the system and keyed in 'Operation GoldStar.' She was curious. An old operation it might be, but it had relevance to the Blake investigation. A message flashed onto her screen telling her she did not have access. The files were password protected. Damn Kenton!

Elwyn knocked on the office door. "Is this the Baslow case or the Wignall one you're mulling over?"

"Does it make a difference?"

"You know it does. Wignall was involved in the trafficking and you should hand over everything we've got to

Kenton. You're chancing it, Rachel. Kenton is bound to find out soon and then he'll blow."

"Find out what exactly? We know nothing. Wignall's dead, he took Baslow's place, we've every right to poke about in his life."

Elwyn put a sheet of paper on her desk. "The information on Woodsmoor from Companies House. It gives the full names and addresses of the three shareholders. Baslow and Longhurst we know," he tapped the sheet. "Now we have Graham's."

"Have you managed to speak to him?" she asked.

"No, there's no phone number. He lives in Hyde. I thought we'd use the element of surprise. You and me should have a ride out there and speak to him personally."

Not what Rachel wanted to do. She'd have preferred to find out more about the goings on at the nursing home, but that would have to wait.

"Okay, you win. But why those two men swapped identities is important to the murders we're investigating, and I'll get to the bottom of it."

* * *

DC Jonny Farrell was on his way to the Hawthorne Nursing Home. Pollard Street was just round the corner from the station, so he'd decided to walk. The fresh air would clear his head. It'd been a long night. He hadn't said too much to his colleagues but at one point the medics weren't sure that his dad would make it. Fortunately, Bobby Farrell was a strong man and he'd rallied. However, there was still a problem. His heart had stopped and he'd been without oxygen for a brief period. Currently the doctors had him under sedation but they couldn't say how he'd be once he came round. There was a real possibility that he'd suffered brain damage. The idea of not getting his father back the way he was terrified Jonny. Bobby Farrell was a larger than life character. He took charge, liked to rule the lives of those close to him, not that he got away with that where Jonny was concerned.

He was met by Pat Wentworth who was keen to set some ground rules. "Say what you like to the staff, but I don't want the residents upsetting. Francis wasn't well known but he was one of them. Most know what's happened and it's cast a cloud over the place."

Jonny wasn't surprised. After all, one of their number had been murdered. "Was there a particular member of staff who took care of Francis regularly?"

"Yes, Kirsty Mallory, but she's not here. Hasn't been in for a day or so. I intend to ring her later, find out what's going on."

"Given what's happened, didn't you think that was suspicious?" Jonny asked.

"Kirsty can be like that, she's a little casual about the job, but the residents like her."

"Do we have her details?"

"Yes. I emailed everything to your boss," Pat Wentworth said.

"In that case, I'll concentrate on the residents. Who do you think will be most helpful?" he asked.

"There's a number of them sitting in the lounge at the bottom of the corridor. Any of them may be able to help, but make sure you speak to Winnie. She might be in her nineties and can't get about much, but she's mentally fit and very alert. When Francis first came here, she tried very hard to get him to integrate. There's not much she misses. She has the room across the corridor from Francis. If anything was going on with him, she'll know."

"Did they speak a lot?" he asked.

"Winnie is the type who speaks to you whether you want to converse or not. She'd be the one doing the talking. I doubt she got much out of Francis in return. A word of advice. I wouldn't muddy the waters by telling them about the swapping identities thing. They might not understand and it'll just confuse the issue."

Pat Wentworth led the way to a large sitting room, where a group of elderly men and women sat sipping tea.

"Come in, love," one of them called out. "You'll be the policeman we're all waiting for."

"That's Winnie," Pat Wentworth whispered.

Wearing light blue trousers and a matching knitted jumper, Winnie sat by the window. "I've never been interviewed by the police before. Are you a detective?"

Jonny retrieved his warrant card from his jacket pocket and showed it to her and the others.

"I'm hoping you can help me," Jonny said to them all. "We're investigating what happened to Francis."

"You want to know who murdered him, you mean," a man said. "Don't wrap it up, lad. Tell it like it is. We're not children. He were done in while he lay asleep in his bed. It could be any one of us next."

"What's your name?" asked Jonny.

"Harold."

"Well, Harold, I doubt that'll happen. Our killer is after specific people, and he kills because of some twisted reason of his own."

"I can't sleep. Had to increase them pills I take. I'm like all these here." He gestured at the small group. "We just want it to end."

It was perfectly understandable. The murder had upset them all. "Does anyone have anything they want to tell me about Francis? It doesn't matter how small or how insignificant you think it is."

There was a universal shaking of heads, apart from Winnie, who beckoned him over.

Jonny sat down beside her. "Do you know something, Winnie?"

She shook her head. "Truth is, you haven't got a clue why he were killed, have you? Pat told me as much. She said you want to speak to us lot because you don't know what happened that night." She leaned in closer to Jonny and whispered, "Well, I'll tell you this much — he were scared, Francis were. Ever since he came here, he thought something like this might happen, and that's why he gave it to me."

Jonny leaned forward. "Gave you what, Winnie?"

She nudged him. "The envelope of course. He said he wanted it somewhere safe in case, and that if anything should happen to him, to give it to the police."

"Do you still have it?" asked Jonny. This could be the breakthrough they were looking for. The envelope had to contain something Francis thought might point to his killer.

"Of course I do. I'm not some doddery old fool, you know." Winnie leaned over and rummaged in her handbag. "Here. I've been looking after this ever since Francis arrived."

Jonny put on a pair of nitrile gloves and examined the plain brown envelope for a few seconds, then started to put it into an evidence bag.

"No you don't," Winnie said. "I want to see what's in there. I've not looked after it all these weeks just to have you snatch the excitement away."

Jonny wasn't sure if he should show her. This was important evidence. "I should give it to my DCI straight away."

"A little peek, that's all. Let's see what Francis was all fired up about."

Jonny was curious himself. He carefully peeled the envelope open and took out what it contained. It wasn't much, just a single solitary photograph, showing three men standing in front of the Midland Hotel in Manchester. One he recognised instantly — it was Danulescu. The other two were facing each other, heads together. The quality was poor, and he could make out one — Ronan Blake — but not the other. It looked as if the photo had been taken from some distance away. Jonny took his mobile from his jacket pocket and took a quick snap of it, put the envelope and photo into an evidence bag and labelled it.

"Thanks, Winnie," he said. "You've done well. I think this could be important."

CHAPTER FIFTEEN

Amy needed to sort the business with Connor Young quickly. Despite having rung in sick, she decided to go into work after all. She'd make out she was feeling better and was concerned about leaving them in the lurch, given how busy they were. She smiled to herself — the DCI would think her a proper little trooper. But the truth was, Amy wanted to suss out where she might find that photo.

She'd no sooner parked up than Jonny knocked on her window. "Thought you were sick. What're you doing in?"

She smiled up at him. "You need me. I'll be fine as long as I don't eat anything."

"Night on the lash, was it?"

Her colleagues knew her so well. "I think it was a sandwich I had here yesterday."

"You want to be careful," Jonny said. "Don't touch the ones with prawns, that's my advice."

"What've you been up to?" she asked.

"Interviewing a group of old folks at the care home," he said.

"Sounds like a hoot. Get anything?"

"I did actually. A photo Wignall gave one of them for safe keeping."

Amy sprang to attention. It had to be the one Connor Young had been on about.

"Give us a look then."

"It's in my boot with some other stuff."

Stella came out of the station entrance and called across to them. "Tell DCI King I'll be back in an hour or so, she knows about my dentist's appointment."

Stella and Jonny stood discussing the joys of dental treatment long enough to allow Amy to take a look into the open boot of his car. On top of a pile of papers was an evidence bag containing a brown envelope with the word 'Police' written on it. After a quick glance to make sure Jonny's attention was elsewhere, Amy stuffed the envelope into her pocket.

Stella drove away, and Jonny grabbed the paperwork from his boot and joined Amy. "I'm on the soft option," he told her. "I've been up most of the night sitting with my dad. Thankfully he's rallied, so panic over."

"Talking to a load of OAPs is hardly the soft option. I bet most of them have no idea what day it is," Amy said.

"One of them, Winnie, was great — in her nineties but still very bright." Struggling to keep a heavy file from slipping out from under his arm, together with the loose paperwork, Jonny stumbled over the steps leading up to the main doors. The lot hit the floor. The loose papers scattered all over the car park, before the wind blew them away.

Amy couldn't believe her luck, the gods were really on her side. When Jonny discovered that the evidence bag containing the envelope with the photo was missing, he'd blame it on the wind.

* * *

The address Rachel and Elwyn had for Sam Graham was on Dowson Road in Hyde. The house was a large redbrick detached, set back off the main road.

"Nice," Elwyn remarked. "Graham did okay for himself by the looks of it. I wouldn't mind something like this myself."

"Too big and far too expensive," Rachel said.

"That's right, dash my dreams. But you're right, and it's not convenient for work either. Living at my sister's is great, it's just around the corner. A house has come on sale just up from hers and I'm seriously considering it."

"And Marie?"

Elwyn shrugged. "She's my ex-wife now and her own woman. She's tight-lipped about her plans, but I know she's got something up her sleeve. I've lived with her long enough to work out how her mind works, but she's telling me nothing."

Rachel gave him a knowing look. "You know what that means, don't you? Another man." Elwyn didn't have time to reply. Rachel's attention was caught by a face peering out of a downstairs front window. "We've been clocked. Come on."

A woman met them at the door. "Mrs Graham?" Rachel asked.

"Yes. Who are you?"

"DCI King and DS Pryce from East Manchester serious crime. Can we have a word?"

The woman stood aside to let them in. "Serious crime? What on earth do you think I've done?"

"Sam Graham lives here, I believe. Is he in?"

"Sam is my son, and he's away," she said quickly.

"We really do need to speak to him, Mrs Graham. Do you have his contact details — his mobile number for example?"

"Why? Can't you discuss whatever it is with me? Sam's working, he won't thank you for interrupting him."

"That can't be helped," Rachel said. Time to be candid. "Mrs Graham, it's possible that Sam is in danger. People he used to work with have been killed, and we're concerned that your son is next on the list."

Her eyes darted from one detective to the other. She was nervous, evidently unsure of what to tell them. "Danger, you say? You're sure of that?"

"Yes," Rachel confirmed. "Sam used to work with Alison Longhurst and Francis Baslow, didn't he?"

"Alison, yes, but they never actually met Baslow. He was a silent partner in the business. To be honest, he wasn't a very nice man. He set targets which were impossible to reach. I kept telling Sam to give it up, but he never listens to me."

"This was the country retirement business, the bungalows?" Elwyn said.

"Yes, although the way it was described was an exaggeration. I saw the piece of land, it was tiny. Sam was involved in nothing but a scam to relieve the unwary of their money. They concentrated on the elderly, retired market, promising a luxury bolthole in the country. He and Alison had pamphlets, brochures and reports that showed how the place would look once it was complete. Sam hated the job in the end, Alison too. He knew that sooner or later they'd come unstuck. He warned Alison and tried to tell Baslow, but apparently he was having none of it. Sam said Baslow threatened them both. My Sam's a big bloke, scared of nowt, but Baslow had him rattled."

"Did Sam and Alison do anything about the threats?" Rachel asked.

"They told Baslow they were done, finished, but he wouldn't have it, said they were up to their necks in it just like him." Mrs Graham hesitated, as if on the verge of divulging something important.

"We're police, Mrs Graham, you have to trust us," Rachel said. "Tell us where your son is and we'll look after you both."

"He read in the paper about that man who was killed and mistaken for Baslow, the one in the nursing home. He knew then that Baslow wants him dead too. When you've caught Baslow, perhaps he'll show himself."

"Your son thinks that Baslow is the killer?" Elwyn asked.

"Yes, he does. He reckons it's just the sort of stunt Baslow would pull — and all the money is missing. The company account was cleared out three months ago."

"Where is Sam, Mrs Graham?" Rachel asked. "We have to speak to him."

"I tried contacting him earlier today but I got nowhere. The mobile number he gave me used to work but now it just goes to voice mail."

Rachel asked. "Can I have it? I'll speak to him myself, impress upon him the need to come forward."

Mrs Graham scribbled the number on Rachel's card and handed it over.

"If you do get hold of him, tell him to phone me."

CHAPTER SIXTEEN

"What d'you think?" Elwyn said.

"She's lying," Rachel said. "Covering for her son. I think she knows very well where he is."

"You don't know that."

Elwyn might have his doubts but Rachel trusted her instincts. "What is interesting is *why* she lied. She's attempting to shift the blame onto Baslow, and we know he's not the killer."

"How so?" Elwyn asked.

"For starters, the confetti. I can't make sense of that at all. And ask yourself, why would Baslow kill Wignall? It gains him nothing. All it does is draw attention to the swap. Leave Wignall to die of his illness and there's no need to have his identity confirmed, and from what the medics say, that wouldn't have been long. His daughter, and us, might have been none the wiser. All we know about Baslow for sure is that he's missing."

"The money, Rachel, what about that? Perhaps Wignall threatened Baslow, wanted a cut. As for his identity, it could well have been the vicar and not his daughter who confirmed it. The confetti thing could be a red herring, his way of throwing us off the track."

"No, I don't buy it, Elwyn. Baslow is missing and so is the money from the Woodsmoor account. For reasons of his own, Baslow wanted to disappear and have everyone believe he's dead, and that's why he's never touched his own bank account, he doesn't need to. Until we can prove otherwise, Sam Graham is a person of interest from now on. He could be our killer."

"Wouldn't he know Wignall wasn't Baslow?" Elwyn asked.

"They never met — Sam's mother just told us that. Baslow kept in the background, it was Sam and Alison who did all the work. Right. Back to the station, see what the others have got, if anything, then I think we should call it a day."

Elwyn nodded. "I'm going to view that house tonight, want to come?"

"I'd better get home. The girls need some input from me. Leave them to their own devices for too long and it takes some sorting."

"Have you requested time off for that wedding?" he asked.

"Not yet, I'm waiting for the right moment. But with this case dragging on, I won't hold my breath. Kenton won't like me leaving you in it."

* * *

Rachel sensed it the moment she walked in. The office buzzed with tension.

"Can I have a word, ma'am?" asked Jonny.

"Can't it wait until tomorrow?" she said wearily.

"I'd rather it didn't," Jonny replied.

"Okay, come into my office."

The young DC looked worried. Rachel assumed it had something to do with his dad. She was wrong.

"I've messed up, ma'am, big-time," he said. "I spoke to the residents at the nursing home like you wanted. One of them, Winnie, had spent time with Wignall. He'd given her an envelope to give to us if anything happened to him. It was a long brown one with 'Police' written on it."

Rachel was intrigued. What did Wignall want them to know? "Do you have it?"

"That's the problem. I can't find it. There was a photo in the envelope, of three men standing outside the Midland Hotel in Manchester — Ronan Blake, Danulescu and one other, who I didn't recognise."

"What d'you mean you can't find it, Jonny?"

He looked down, shamefaced. "I've lost it. Worse than that, I didn't even notice straight away. I've been so worried about my dad my mind's not been on the job."

This wasn't like Jonny. Ordinarily Rachel would have thrown the kitchen sink at him, but the young DC was under a lot of stress right now. "But you did take a picture of it with your phone?"

Jonny smiled. "Yes, ma'am. I thought that the team here should see it while the envelope was being processed." He handed Rachel his mobile with the image ready for her to see.

"Send me a copy and I'll get it blown up. I reckon Wignall took this. He was into photography — his sister told us. I don't recognise the third man either. I'll get Stella on it."

"I'm really sorry. I never lose things."

"I know, but don't worry, we have the image and that's the important thing." She nodded at him. "Would you mind going back there tomorrow? There's a young carer called Kirsty, who's been off since Wignall's murder. We need to know a lot more about her. If she's still not in work, go to her address."

"We were told about her. I'll go first thing," he said.

As Jonny left her office, Kenton walked in and sat down on the other side of her desk, facing her.

"How's the case going? Caught your killer yet?"

Keeping her eyes on the file she was pretending to read, Rachel said, "No, but we've got several suspects. I'm expecting a breakthrough any day."

"I'll have a look at the file, see if I can help." He held out his hand.

Rachel's head shot up. "Not necessary. You must have more important things to do."

"Not really. I'm a detective not an administrator. Harding's job is all very well but it doesn't suit me."

Rachel smiled. Served him right. She was about to respond when her mobile beeped and Shona's face appeared on the screen. She did not want to talk to her with Kenton earwigging. "Do you mind? I should take this."

But Kenton wasn't going anywhere. He sat back and crossed his legs. "Be my guest."

"It's personal."

He merely shrugged. He clearly had no intention of leaving her office.

With a glare at him, Rachel answered the call. "Can I ring you later, Shona, when I'm home?" Unable to get a word in, Rachel listened to her friend gabble on for several minutes. "I'm still trying to work it out, it'd mean taking time off. Look, we'll speak properly tonight. Bye."

"Need time off? Why didn't you say?" Kenton said.

"Because it's not important and I haven't made my mind up yet."

"Tell me about it. Perhaps I can help."

"An old friend of mine is getting married and she wants me to be a bridesmaid, that's all."

"That sounds pretty important to me. It's a big deal being a bridesmaid," Kenton said.

"Well, she lives in Spain, that's why I can't make it. It isn't just a day out — it'd take two or three."

"When does she need you?" Kenton asked.

"The wedding is three days away — but it's out of the question, this case we're dealing with needs my complete attention."

"Go. I insist. I'll take over the case. DS Pryce is an excellent officer, he'll keep me on track, and I'll be pleased to have something to get my teeth into."

That wasn't the reaction Rachel was expecting, but he obviously meant it. "I can't just swan off," she said weakly.

"It's hardly that, is it? You're owed the time and your HR record shows that you've not taken a break in ages."

He was up to something, Rachel was sure, but she didn't know what, unless it was the trafficking connection that interested him. Time to put that to rest. "You've asked to look at the file, so you'll see that the first victim wasn't the person the killer thought he was. Francis Baslow and a certain Joseph Wignall swapped identities when they left hospital. Wignall, the first victim, was linked to the Blake case. He drove a container lorry across Europe for the traffickers."

"I read the notes on the system so I'm up to date with that little snippet. Mind you, you should have told me. You also searched his house. Find anything?"

"No. Dr Glover will give it the once over, but we do know that someone has been sleeping there."

"Anything else I need to know?" he asked.

Rachel decided to keep the information about the photograph to herself for now. She'd have a quiet word with both Jonny and Elwyn before she left. "No."

CHAPTER SEVENTEEN

Day Five

Rachel had booked her flight and packed a bag the night before and intended to leave for the airport straight from work. Kenton had made going to Spain for the wedding sound so easy, and once she thought about it, Rachel realised he was right. She'd be gone three days tops, and Elwyn would keep a tight hold on the reins.

"Can I come with you?" Megan, her eldest daughter, asked.

"Sorry, it's just me, this time."

"Not fair. You get to go off to Spain and we're stuck here in the rain, up to our ears in homework."

"I won't be sunbathing if that's what you mean. There won't be time. I'll be done up like a fairy on top of a Christmas tree doing my bridesmaid's duties, whatever they are."

"You'll have a great time, as well you know. Bring us something back and take lots of piccies and I might forgive you."

"Make sure you look after Mia and don't give your dad any trouble."

"Chance would be a fine thing. He's practically living at Belinda's now."

"I've had a word. He'll be here while I'm gone."

Once Megan had left the room, Rachel called Jude on her mobile. She wanted to clear up one or two things before she left. No reply, just voice mail. Next, she rang Jason Fox, Jude's second in command. "Where's your leader?"

"Jude's been closeted in that lab of hers since she returned from Stafford. Whatever samples she brought back have had her complete attention. You're stuck with me, I'm afraid. What can I do for you?"

"I asked for Joseph Wignall's house to be gone over — prints, any trace of DNA, usual stuff. Are the results in yet?"

"You're in luck. We found prints belonging to Wignall and his sister, as you'd expect, but there was a third set."

Rachel held her breath. *Not Jed's, please.*

"They belong to a Connor Young. He has a record, been in young offenders and is known to do a bit of dealing."

Rachel breathed out. "And that was it? No other prints?"

"Sorry. I don't know what you were expecting."

"What about Baslow's house — anything there?"

"No, just prints belonging to him and his daughter."

"Thanks, Jason. When Jude surfaces, tell her I'm off to Malaga for a few days, to a friend's wedding. I'll be in touch when I get back."

Mia came in. "When are you catching the plane?"

"Later today, sweetie, but I'm off to work first. Your dad will be here, he'll do tea. I'll ring you the minute I get to Malaga. Tomoz will be a catch-up day with Shona and then the wedding is the day after. Once it's done, I'll be home. Shona and Juan will be off honeymooning in Malta."

"A trip to Spain. You have all the fun."

"With a job like mine, don't I just," Rachel said, giving her youngest a peck on the cheek. She needed to get going, there was a lot to organise before her flight. She had a list of tasks for the team, uppermost of which was finding Sam Graham.

* * *

Jonny Farrell glanced at the address DCI King had given him for Kirsty Mallory and keyed the postcode into his car's satnav. The young woman lived off Hyde Road in West Gorton, not too far away. She still hadn't shown up at work, so hopefully he'd find her there.

Jonny was in a happier frame of mind today. His father had had a better night. The operation and the medication were doing the job. He'd been conscious for a while and, much to Jonny's relief, had seemed like his old self. If he continued to progress, his doctor had said he'd be home by the weekend.

Kirsty hadn't turned up at work at the nursing home for several days now, and hadn't given Pat Wentworth a reason. When Jonny saw the curtains both upstairs and down pulled shut, he suspected that she was lying low. He banged on the front door and then called through the letterbox: "Police!"

After several minutes, the door was opened by a scruffy young man in a track suit. "What's the rush? Nowt happening 'ere. You must 'ave t'wrong house."

"Kirsty Mallory?"

He yelled up the stairs, "Kirst! You're wanted."

Jonny showed him his warrant card. "Who are you?"

"Just a friend, mate. Kirst let me stay over — had a skinful last night, know what I mean?"

"Name?" Jonny said.

"Connor Young."

Hauling a dressing gown around herself, a blonde girl came down the stairs, pushing Young out of the way. She didn't look happy. "What d'you want?"

"I'm DC Farrell, East Manchester CID. You work at Hawthorne Lodge Nursing Home?" The girl nodded. "I'd like to know about the resident called Francis Baslow," Jonny said.

"Except he wasn't, was he?" She grinned. "You see, I knew he was really Joe Wignall."

"And you didn't tell anyone — the owner of the home for example?"

"None of my business, was it? Keep your head down and get on with the work, that's my motto."

"How did you know he was Wignall?"

"I'd seen him around. He used to go to the same pub as me sometimes."

"Did you speak to him about it?" Jonny asked.

"We shared a joke about it. The bloke whose place he took had paid him to do it. Joe were ill, couldn't have managed without care, so the arrangement suited them both. Mind you, he wanted it to stay our secret."

"Did you supply Wignall with heroin?"

Her eyes widened. "What d'you think? I'm not stupid, copper. I stay the right side of the law, me."

"Someone supplied and administered heroin. Track marks were found on his lower legs and he could not have done that himself."

Kirsty stared back at him, hands on hips. "Don't look at me. I never helped him! Have you tackled Wentworth about this?"

"Why haven't you been to work since Joseph died?" he asked.

"I've been ill."

"And you've no idea where the heroin came from?"

She shrugged. "No, and you can't go around blaming everyone who knew him. In a way it's good someone did help. Joe were in a lot of pain, and no one else was doing owt."

Jonny turned to the lad. "What about you, Connor? You do any dealing?"

The question seemed to rattle Kirsty. She looked at Connor and shook her head. "You can't prove owt," she said, not giving Connor a chance to reply. "Connor's never been near the home."

Jonny didn't believe Kirsty Mallory, not for one minute. But he had no proof. There was also the question of the money. Joseph Wignall was supplied with heroin, that was certain, but how did he pay for it? This pair wouldn't do anything without being paid. "Did you ever see Joe with money?"

Kirsty shook her head. "A few coins perhaps, that's all. Certainly not enough to pay for a fix."

"Are you charging us with owt, or what?" Connor asked. "Cause this is getting boring. I've got stuff to do, people to see." He winked.

Jonny had no proof that these two had done anything wrong — except for his instincts. He didn't doubt for one moment that Young knew how to get his hands on any drug he wanted and Kirsty had been Joseph's personal carer. Between the two of them, they could well have had a neat little scam going. "We'll speak again. Don't leave this address without letting the station know."

Without more evidence, he'd get nothing further out of either of them.

* * *

"And he didn't put up a fight?" Elwyn asked.

"No, Elwyn, just said I should go. Mind you, that does mean you're saddled with him, and he wants to be hands on," Rachel said.

"Could be interesting. When are you back?"

"I'm leaving tonight and I'll be back in three days. Believe me, I won't stay away a minute longer than I have to. I've booked an early plane back from Malaga, so I'll come straight in and catch up."

"We'll cope. Don't worry, you go off and enjoy yourself."

"Meanwhile — priorities," she said.

"Finding Sam Graham is uppermost," Elwyn said, "and we need to know what happened to Baslow. On the Graham front, I've been doing some digging. I'm meeting someone later this morning who I hope will be able to help. He was a customer of Woodsmoor and wasn't very happy about the outcome."

"Good work, Elwyn. I'd come with you but I want to sort out some paperwork here before I leave. I also want you to find out all you can about one Connor Young. He's known to deal drugs, and his name has come up."

Elwyn wrote the name on the incident board.

"Incidentally, do you know what Jude was up to in Stafford?" Rachel asked. "I've not been able to contact her since she returned. It all seems very hush-hush."

"Whatever it is, it belongs to Stafford not us," Elwyn said sagely. "We've got enough to sort out. Jude will ring when she's ready."

CHAPTER EIGHTEEN

In his late sixties, Cyril Hardacre was evidently a man who didn't like change. He told them that he'd lived at the same address since getting married forty years ago. His furniture looked like it dated from that period. This made it all the more surprising that he'd risked everything on the strength of a glossy brochure.

"To be honest, I don't know what possessed me. I'm not usually so cavalier. I didn't tell Barbara for weeks, couldn't summon up the courage. I mean, how d'you tell your wife you've lost most of your life savings? It wasn't as if it was just mine either, there was a lump sum from her pension pot too."

Elwyn was drinking tea with Cyril in his sitting room. Mrs Hardacre was out at her weekly church coffee morning. "Tell me how you got drawn in," he asked.

"She caught me unawares. She had all this printed bumf, a beautiful brochure, and was so enthusiastic about the product. Alison was her name. Friendly young woman with an engaging smile. I hid the paperwork from Joyce, my wife, but I did read it through. The place, Woodsmoor, was just what Joyce had always wanted. Our own little idyll in the country, not too far away, and I love fishing. The prices were reasonable too. I thought we'd sell this place and have money left over. Alison said it would be completed and open for occupation within six months. Eventually I plucked up courage and spoke to Joyce about it. She was keen on the idea too, which surprised me."

"How much did you spend?" Elwyn asked.

"The bungalows weren't as expensive as some I've seen, but there was a hefty annual service charge. We paid an initial deposit of twenty grand. We paid more later on. Alison came round and told us that the project was nearly complete and that they'd need another fifty. A couple of our retired friends bought in too." He handed Elwyn a file of paperwork from the coffee table. "This is what she gave us in return for the money." He sighed heavily. "It's all we ever got, an' all."

The paperwork included a brochure, several leaflets about extras and a plan of the site.

"And you didn't suspect that there was anything untoward about the deal, or Alison herself?"

"No, why should I? She showed me a fancy card, it had the office address on it and everything. Allegedly this Woodsmoor site in Cheshire was beautiful, it would have everything we could possibly need. She seemed so nice, so genuine. I trusted her."

"Did you meet anyone else from Woodsmoor?"

"A couple of weeks after we paid the deposit she came back with a bloke. Big chap he was, didn't say much. Alison introduced him as Sam. Joyce said he was a bit intimidating but he was well-mannered enough."

"What did they want?" asked Elwyn.

"She showed us the leaflets about all the extras we could buy into. I told her we'd think about it, but the bloke, Sam, he was quite forceful as I remember. We opted for gym membership and the golf club."

"You could have said no. Sent them packing."

Cyril Hardacre hung his head. "That man made me nervous, and Joyce was keen. Later that same day we transferred more money into Woodsmoor's account. Bloody stupid move. I don't know what possessed me. I haven't seen either of them from that day to this."

"Didn't you engage a solicitor to deal with the conveyancing?" asked Elwyn.

"Alison said they had their own people and that it was included in the price. We thought we were getting a bargain."

Elwyn felt sorry for the elderly man. He'd been well and truly duped.

"I've rung the number on that card she gave me umpteen times. Me and Joyce even took a ride out to the site in Cheshire, but the land was all boarded up. It was nowt but a pocket handkerchief anyway. The company went bust, you see, so there's nothing more to be done."

"Did you complain?" Elwyn asked.

"Yes. I went to you lot and I saw a solicitor, but we'd bought in, parted with our money willingly. The company was genuine, it just had no chance of succeeding."

"No comeback, then?"

Cyril shook his head. "That's what we believed, but then I saw the ad in the paper, about the meeting."

"And you went along?"

"Both me and Joyce. There were a lot of angry people there, I can tell you. Threatening, name calling, and more swearing than I've heard in years. Folk were angry, desperate to find Alison Longhurst and Sam Graham, but no one knew where they'd gone. One man said there was a silent partner behind the business and that he was the real boss, the brains behind the scam." Cyril nodded. "By this time that's what everyone believed, that we'd been scammed."

"Do you know the names of any of the other people who bought into Woodsmoor?"

"Yes. We agreed to stay in touch and keep each other informed if anything changed. We have a WhatsApp group, there's about twenty of us in it." He looked at Elwyn, shaking his head sadly. "Some scam, eh? They made a fortune out of us lot."

"This group of yours. You were all clearly upset, but was anyone more aggressive than the rest?"

"We were all bloody pissed-off, I can tell you. That company got thousands out of us. I couldn't say how anyone in particular felt. Emotions were running high and people say things, don't they?"

"Could I have access to the group, and names if you've got them. They'll all have to be contacted," Elwyn said.

"Has something happened? Is there a chance we'll get our money back?"

Cyril Hardacre obviously didn't know. He mustn't have read the local paper recently. "Alison Longhurst and a man the killer thought to be Francis Baslow, the silent partner, have been murdered."

* * *

"Jonny is speaking to a couple who may have supplied drugs to Wignall — Kirsty Mallory, a carer from Hawthorne Lodge and her boyfriend, Connor Young. He's got form and his prints were found in Wignall's house," Rachel said to Amy. "He's spoken to both of them but they're saying nothing, and until we have something concrete it's no use hauling them in. That's what I want you to look at. I want the home searching, particularly Wignall's room, and get more background on the pair."

Amy's face turned pale. "Connor Young, ma'am. I know him."

Rachel was already running late. If she was to get to the airport in time for her flight, this had to go smooth. "What difference does that make? In what context do you know him? Is there something else? If so, out with it, Amy. I haven't got time for riddles."

The young DC appeared to be struggling for words. "I've done something, ma'am. Connor will want to save his skin, so if he's arrested, he'll tell you and make it sound ten times worse than it is."

Rachel closed her eyes. What now? "Come into my office. Sit down and tell me what's going on."

"I've been stupid, ma'am. I have a brother, Aiden, he's a user, been addicted for a long time and can't get clean. Connor Young supplies him."

"I'm not liking the sound of this."

"Sorry, ma'am, but you need to know. Connor has threatened both me and Aiden. He's a bad 'un, and is more than capable of doing us real harm."

"Okay, your brother is an addict, but how are you mixed up with him?"

"Young approached me, and we met up. He wanted me to get something for him. Said if I did what he asked he'll wipe Aiden's debt." Amy looked away. "For all I know, my stupid brother owes him thousands."

"Is that it? You're worried about your brother's safety?"

"Aiden is a mess. He's not always able to get what he needs for himself."

This could be bad. "What hold does he have over you?" Rachel asked. "Tell me now, I don't want any surprises in the interview room."

"Connor knows that I've occasionally got stuff for Aiden too. I know people, dealers and such. That's what makes him so persuasive. He's threatened to shop me."

Rachel was angry. "You're a bloody fool, d'you know that? Tell me, what did Young want from you?"

Amy handed Rachel the photo. "This. I took it from the boot of Jonny's car. He dropped his stuff in the car park and presumed it had blown away."

Rachel waved the thing in her face. "Jonny thinks he lost this! He came and apologised to me. He was really upset."

"I'm sorry, ma'am, but I didn't know what to do. Connor said he'd half kill Aiden if I didn't get it for him."

Rachel studied the photo. It had to be important. She pointed to the man with Blake and Danulescu. "Do you know who this is?"

"No, ma'am, but I bet Connor does."

Perhaps he did, but it wouldn't be Amy asking him. "You'll have to keep out of it. I'll decide what to do with you when I get back. I'm going to have them both brought in, Young and that girlfriend of his. In the meantime, help Elwyn with the research into Woodsmoor and the disgruntled customers. And do not go near Connor Young. Do you understand?"

The clock ticking, Rachel now needed a word with Elwyn. He wasn't in the office so she rang his mobile.

"I'm grabbing a bite in the canteen. What is it?"

"I want Connor Young and Kirsty bringing in for questioning as soon as. Young deals drugs and he pressurised Amy to hand over a piece of evidence."

"What evidence?"

"A photo that Wignall wanted passing on to us. It's Blake, Danulescu and another man I don't recognise. It has to be important in some way. I'll text you the image. It strikes me that Wignall could have been hoarding other stuff, do another search of his place see what you can find."

"We've a case of our own to investigate," he reminded her. "Give the photo to Kenton and have done with it. If he finds out that you've kept evidence from him, he won't be happy."

"Wignall is part of our case too. He swapped places with Baslow, remember? Just do it, Elwyn. Look at Wignall's place one last time and see what you turn up."

CHAPTER NINETEEN

Rachel took a taxi to the airport. She sat back, closed her eyes and tried to relax as it sped along the motorway, but her head was full of the case. Elwyn had returned, delivered a summary of what Cyril Hardacre had told him and agreed to keep her briefed on events while she was away. All very well but it should be her holding the reins. This was the break they'd been looking for, and she wanted to speak to Hardacre herself. He could be holding vital information that would help them. Their killer was more than likely lurking in that WhatsApp group. Rachel had left tech support, with Elwyn, getting the names and addresses so they could make a start on the follow-up. Rachel told Jonny the photo had turned up in the car park, which was quite feasible. She'd also told him to bring in Connor Young and Kirsty. Hopefully he'd find out who the unknown man in the photo was. A few days away and she might just return to some answers.

"Going somewhere nice?" the driver asked.

"Spain, for a wedding." Saying it out loud stirred up some excitement, and the problems of the case melted a little. Shona knew how to enjoy herself, and she always threw a good party. The wedding would be crazy, and knowing how well-heeled Juan was, there'd be no expense spared. Rachel wondered how many other friends from uni she'd found and invited.

"No luggage?" the driver asked as he dropped her off.

Rachel smiled. "Travel light, that's my motto." Everything she needed was in her hand luggage. Anything else, she'd borrow off Shona. From her posts on Facebook, she had a wardrobe to die for. The bridesmaid dress was sorted too. Shona had sent details of what she wanted and Rachel had had a fitting at a bridal shop in Manchester weeks ago. The dress was now waiting for her at Shona's villa in Spain. It was sweet of her that she had put everything in place without even knowing for certain whether Rachel could go.

Rachel had already checked in online and negotiating security at the airport was relatively quick. Finally, she was sipping a gin and tonic in the lounge before take-off. Bliss.

* * *

"We know the taxi firm was Bolton's. I'm hoping that we can find the driver and he remembers something useful," Jonny said.

Amy sat in the passenger seat of Jonny's car. "There might be paperwork, computer records, then we can get the driver from there."

"They know we're coming. From what we've been told, the real Baslow got a taxi and so did Wignall."

"Who waited with him? Do we know?"

"The ward sister presumes it was a porter, but she's no idea which one. We'll make this the last job of the day. We can't do anything with the information Elwyn brought back from Hardacre until we have the names." He pulled out of the car park onto the main road. "What did the boss drag you into her office for?"

How to answer that one? "Nothing really. She wants me to get on top of my paperwork while she's gone. A bit of a pep talk, that's all." Amy smiled.

"You sure? You've been off. Not been up to anything, have you?"

"What d'you take me for! I was sick, dodgy sandwich, remember. You've got some cheek, Farrell! The boss wants a chat and you're quick off the mark with the third degree. We can't all be teacher's pet, you know!"

Jonny was taken aback. "That's not what I am at all. She's alright, is Rachel. She's been very good with me while my dad's been ill."

"Your face fits better than mine. Make the most of it. She's a moody cow, I'm sure it won't last."

They travelled the rest of the way in silence. Jonny had no wish to say anything else that would have Amy jumping down his throat.

When they arrived at the taxi depot, Amy got out of the car without saying a word.

"We need to find whoever is in charge. The office is that way," Jonny pointed.

"I've been here before," Amy retorted.

"Can I help, mate?" a man asked.

Jonny showed the man his badge. "We're after some information about a patient picked up from Wythenshawe three months ago."

"Transfer, was it? We get a lot of them."

"Yes, to a nursing home," Amy said.

"Which one?"

"Hawthorne Lodge in Ancoats," said Jonny.

"That's the place where that bloke got himself murdered."

"Yes," Amy said. "So if there's anything you can tell us . . ."

He called out to a man standing in the corner of the room making coffee. "Bob! These want a word." He looked at the detectives. "Bob's your man. Does all the Hawthorne jobs, lives just round the corner. He read about it in the paper, it shook him up. He remembers the bloke."

Bob came over — he'd obviously overheard the conversation. "I remember because he was so sick. Should have been taken in an ambulance if you ask me."

"Did you see the man waiting with him?"

"He was a weird one. The pair seemed friendly, and I asked if we could drop him off somewhere, but he refused. We got on our way but the bloke I picked up had forgotten to pick up his meds, so we had to go back. I had a ten minute wait in the pharmacy, put me right out. When I got back to the cab the other bloke was climbing into a car, it weren't no cab either. Some scally was driving it, big lad in a tracksuit. We were stuck at that roundabout near the pick-up point. I can't be sure but I think the bloke handed the lad a wad of cash, certainly looked like that to me. I did ask my fare if the other bloke was okay but he said not to worry."

"This lad, do you know him?"

"No, but I have seen him since. He knocks around with the lass from Hawthorne. Kirsty's her name."

Jonny had a pretty good idea who he was talking about. It had to be Connor Young.

"Thanks," Amy said. "That's really helpful."

"We drag them in," Jonny said as they walked back to the car.

Amy shook her head. "I bet we'll get nowt from either of them. Past masters at running rings around police, that pair."

CHAPTER TWENTY

It was an uneventful flight, and Rachel had the added bonus of not having to wait at the luggage carousel in Malaga. All Rachel had to do now was find the lift Shona had promised. On her way out of the airport, she rang home. The girls were fine, Alan was in attendance and Belinda was staying over. She smiled to herself. It was good he'd found someone. She didn't feel quite so guilty about leaving them now.

She spotted him at once, positioned by the main doorway and holding a large placard in the air with the name 'King' printed on it. Shona didn't do things by halves.

She smiled at him. "Hi, I'm Rachel King. You must be my lift."

He nodded. "The car is just outside. May I take your case, madam?"

He was nice, and so was the car, roomy, with plush seats and tinted windows.

Just as she was about to clamber in, he said, "Ms Cassells will phone you later."

That confused Rachel. Why wasn't Shona waiting for her? It'd been years for goodness sake! "Aren't we going to her villa?"

"There's been a change of plan. Ms Cassells said you'd understand."

Well, she was wrong on that score. It'd been a long, tiring day and all Rachel wanted was to put her feet up. She was about to ask where she was being taken — hopefully not to some touristy hotel or event — when a man she hadn't spotted leaned forward out of the shadows in the rear of the car.

"Get in, Rachel, and leave Khalid be."

For one heart stopping moment everything around her fell silent. Rachel was momentarily struck dumb. What was Jed doing here? And then everything fell into place like the last pieces of a jigsaw puzzle. She'd been set up. This was down to the pair of them, Jed and Shona. They'd organised this between them.

"We're blocking the way. We should leave before we draw attention to ourselves," Khalid urged.

Reluctantly, Rachel clambered into the rear of the car and sat next to Jed. "Is this your doing? I wouldn't put it past you. Is there even a wedding?"

"Oh there's to be a wedding alright," he said. "Shona has done nothing but fuss over the details for weeks."

"She said nothing to me about you being here. What's going on?"

"All in good time, Rachel. You'll have your catch-up with Shona tomorrow. Tonight, she and Juan are entertaining Juan's parents and extended family, so she's asked me to look after you."

Rachel felt betrayed. But she wasn't stupid. Whatever he said, Jed would have had a hand in this. There was nothing she could do and the prospect of storming off and finding some strange hotel didn't appeal. She'd just have to accept things as they were. "You've been gone a while, and you're doing okay from the look of things. Life in the sun suits you."

Jed grunted. "That's a matter of opinion. The truth is, I'm bored stiff. All I've done for weeks is potter around on the boat and work on my tan."

"Boat?"

"Well, more a yacht really. It belongs to Ahmed, Khalid's brother. He very kindly said I could stay on it while I'm here. That's where we're going now."

Just like him to fall on his feet. "Whatever you're up to, you look like a man without a care in the world which, given your recent history, is a long way from the truth." She lowered her voice so Khalid couldn't hear. "You're a wanted man, Jed, d'you know that?"

"It'll come right," he said nonchalantly. "You don't think I'm guilty, do you, Rachel?" He turned to face her. "I'm relying on you of all people to trust me."

"Trust you? I've been watching your back for weeks. My colleagues, my current boss, the world and his wife in fact, all think you were behind the trafficking scam."

"And you?"

"No, of course not. I know you better than that, Jed McAteer. But the whole case has thrown me. Mark Kenton is my new boss. Can you imagine what that's like? He hates you with a passion. He's got a hefty file on your past misdemeanours and reckons you're in the frame for the trafficking case. He's determined to get you for it. You should be more careful, coming to an airport. You might be seen."

Laughing at her outburst, Jed shook his head. "I'm sure it's not that bad. He can't be trying very hard. I've not seen any police, private investigators or anyone since I've been away."

"Well, you be careful while I'm here. I can't afford to be caught with you," she said. "You might think this is one huge joke, but it's my job we're talking about here."

"Calm down, Rachel, nothing is going to happen. You will go to Shona's wedding, have a great time, and return home. A few hours spent with me is hardly going to make any difference."

"Where's this yacht?"

"A few miles along the coast at Puerto Banus."

This was an upmarket resort next to Marbella. Rachel had read about it in the holiday brochures. "Very swish. Must cost a fortune to moor it there."

"Ahmed can afford it, believe me," Jed said. "We should arrive in about half an hour. We'll eat and then tonight Khalid will cruise to the marina in Malaga. Tomorrow morning he'll take you to Shona's villa."

Fair enough. One night and then she'd be free of the worry of having him around. Whether he took it seriously or not, Jed was a risky commodity. There was a European warrant out for his arrest. If he should be apprehended while she was with him, it would difficult to explain.

"How's my daughter?"

"Mia is fine and please don't call her that. She's Alan's daughter."

"How long d'you think you can keep that up? I bet she's asking questions."

"Yes, and I've put her straight." She looked out of the window.

"Sooner or later, Rachel, we'll all have to come to terms with the truth."

She knew that, but there was no rush. Mia could get a few more years under her belt first. "I'll decide when that is, and I'd be grateful if you kept out of it."

"We'll see what happens first. I won't lie to her though. If Mia asks me, I'll tell her the truth."

This made Rachel's stomach churn. Jed telling Mia the truth might end the convenient domestic arrangement she had with Alan.

They had reached the waterfront. "We're here," Jed announced. "See that huge silver job? That's Ahmed's."

The craft glistened in the last of the evening sun. It was beautiful, with sleek lines, twice the size of its neighbours. "That's some yacht. What does he do, this friend of yours? Nothing dodgy I hope."

"He's in property — selling to the Brits, in Spain and Portugal mostly. He made the big money twenty years ago, and today he lives by investing wisely."

"It's spectacular. I've never been anywhere like this before," Rachel said.

Khalid took her case and Jed led the way on board. "We'll eat soon. There's a great restaurant along the road. The chef will send something over."

Rachel stood on the deck and looked at her surroundings. The marina was full. An absolute fortune in yachts bobbed up and down with hardly any space between them. Across the narrow road shops and eateries were lined up, all of them still open. She noted the designer names above the shops — you'd have to been very well-heeled to shop here. Jed had obviously not suffered during his time away, he was living in the lap of luxury. Rachel smiled to herself. Just like him.

CHAPTER TWENTY-ONE

It was time for Sam Graham to die. After all, the police were expecting such an outcome, so it would be a shame to disappoint. The planning stage was complete but things would be a little different this time. The police would put that down to Graham being a big bloke and, unlike the other two, well able to handle himself.

He'd been keeping an eye on his target for several days and had his habits down pat. He'd even spoken to him a couple of times and reckoned it wouldn't take much to get him to believe the story. The fool was always looking for a way to make an easy crust. The target would see him as someone he could dupe, scam money from, a mistake many had made, and paid for.

He had followed his target to a car park, late that Thursday night. The perfect time. The facility was closed on Fridays so the body wouldn't be discovered until Monday — long enough to muddy the waters forensically.

"Got a light?" He called out to his prey, and caught the lighter thrown to him. "Don't know a good mechanic, do you? My car won't start and I can't get a reply from my rescue service."

"Sorry, mate, no idea," the man said.

"Don't suppose you'd give me a push? It might be nothing more than a flat battery."

The other came forward and positioned himself at the rear of the car. "Get behind the wheel then. I've not got all night."

A smile flickered across the killer's face. "I'll get behind the wheel." He walked round to the front, reached in the car and picked up a crowbar from the floor. It was dark in the car park, and his victim was bent over, head down. He'd never notice. Perfect.

* * *

"Forensics have been through Wignall's house once already, and they didn't find anything untoward," Jonny complained.

"We don't have much choice. Rachel wants us to go over it again. We know Wignall was into photography, he snapped the picture of the three men. There might be other important stuff that was missed. He did work for Blake, remember."

"So we search, but we don't know what for, and it's not even relevant to our own case?"

"That's about the size of it," Elwyn said soberly. "We'll do what we can. Anything that sheds light on the identity of the third man in that photo will do for starters."

Jonny shook his head. "An impossible task if you ask me."

"We won't waste too much time — a quick search and then we'll call it a day. Tomorrow first thing, we'll bring Young and his girlfriend in for a chat."

They pulled up outside the house. The searches being complete, it had been closed up, but now the front door was swinging in the breeze.

"Uninvited guests," said Jonny.

"A rundown area," Elwyn said. "Could be someone dossing down for the night. We know that Young used it for that."

The house had been in a state the first time Elwyn had seen it, but whoever had been here since had completely trashed the place. The bin bags and boxes had been emptied onto the floor and what little furniture there was had been broken up.

Jonny nodded to the remnants of a fire in the hearth. "Whoever did this didn't rush. There's even a smell of cooked bacon."

"Connor Young again perhaps. We'll ask him in the morning," Elwyn said.

"Where do we start?" Jonny asked, looking around.

"This little lot has been turned upside down, so not in here. Wignall was the careful type. He gave your old lady that photo for safekeeping, so anything else he didn't want finding will be well hidden."

"Why not give that over for safe keeping too?"

"I dunno. We're not mind readers."

With a loud sigh, Jonny trudged upstairs. Minutes later he shouted down, "Nothing but empty rooms up here, guv."

Elwyn carefully picked his way around the boxes in the living room. "Are there any wardrobes?"

"There's some old fitted cupboards," Jonny said.

"Look at them then and I'll do the kitchen."

The kitchen was furnished with an old Calor gas stove, one wall cupboard and a table. There was no cellar and no back garden. Elwyn went upstairs to join Jonny. "There's nowhere to hide anything down there."

"Up here neither." He nodded at one of the cupboards. "The doors are hanging off that one. If Wignall had anything, he must have stashed it somewhere else."

Elwyn was looking at the ancient battered cupboards. "We had these in the house I grew up in — old-fashioned and fitted into the alcoves either side of the fireplace. They might look like a solid job but there's usually a space under the base."

"I'd have missed that. How did you know?" Jonny asked.

"When I was a kid, I hid anything I didn't want my parents to find under the base of cupboards similar to these."

Was it the same here? Jonny ran his hand over the cupboard floor, feeling for any way of lifting it up. "This is loose," he said. "I can lift the base of this one right out."

"Told you Wignall was a canny chap."

Jonny felt around underneath and his hand touched a plastic bag. He lifted it out and set it down.

"Careful," Elwyn said. "That's a laptop. There has to be important stuff on it or Wignall wouldn't have hidden it. We'll get this to forensics right away."

"There's another bag here, full of personal stuff, letters and the like. We'll take that too, go through it. You get off home," Jonny said. "I'll take this little lot in."

CHAPTER TWENTY-TWO

Day Six

As Rachel slowly woke up, the light hit her right between the eyes. She rubbed her head, it hurt like hell. Too much wine the night before, but there was worse. She was lying in Jed's bed. She'd made a first-class fool of herself. Sleeping with him had been the last thing on her mind, but that's exactly what had happened. Too much alcohol? Too tired to resist her attraction? Rachel knew these were just excuses. The truth was, her willpower was zero when it came to Jed.

She was alone, but could hear voices outside on the deck. Rachel had no idea where they were. She been vaguely aware of the craft moving during the night and presumed they were no longer moored at Puerto Banus.

Though it was just a boat, the bedroom was the height of luxury. On the run or not, Jed certainly lived in style. She checked her mobile — gone ten o'clock. Rachel couldn't remember the last time she'd slept this late.

"If you look out of that window, you'll see the marina at Malaga."

Jed entered the room, bent down and kissed her cheek. He put a mug of coffee on the cabinet beside her. "Khalid will moor the yacht and then I'll take you somewhere special for breakfast. What d'you fancy?"

"I couldn't eat a thing," she said. "I need to get organised. Shona must be wondering what's happened to me."

"It's still early."

"I need to get up and get to Shona's," Rachel said.

"I thought we'd spend the morning together. I'll show you around Malaga, do some shopping. I still need to buy the happy couple a present."

"You're coming to the wedding?" Rachel had assumed that Jed wouldn't want to be seen in public. Juan was a well-known businessman and the press might be present, there'd certainly be photographers, and a picture might make its way into the local paper.

"Of course. Me, you . . . Shona's even invited Liam. It'll be like old times."

"Things are different now, Jed. Don't you kid yourself that what happened last night has changed anything. I'm still a detective, and you're still a wanted man."

Jed gave her an odd look. "Sometimes I think you believe all that rubbish about me, Rachel. You should have more faith. I admit I was a wrong 'un once, but that was a long time ago. This last decade I've built a successful business and changed my ways. Put simply, I'm not the man you knew when we were young."

She looked into his eyes. Was he telling the truth? Had he really left the past behind? Rachel had never wanted to believe him more than at this moment. But there was no time for a discussion now. "Do you mind? I want to get up and sort myself out."

"Be my guest," he said. "I'll wait for you on deck."

Rachel hated herself for being so 'off' with him. But how was she supposed to act? He'd virtually hijacked her, and now he wanted to monopolise her time. She wasn't sure whether to unpack — would she be coming back here or staying at Shona's?

She showered and put on a strappy dress and sandals. "I'm sorry," she said, joining Jed on deck. "I know you weren't part of the trafficking gang, but I'm in an impossible position. My boss thinks you're up to your eyes in it and I don't have evidence to prove otherwise."

Jed winked at her. "You've got it wrong. Your boss doesn't think anything of the sort. True, he lacks evidence, but it's not me he's after."

Rachel stared. What did he mean? "You know something. Come on, what are you hiding from me? My current boss is Mark Kenton, the man you told me to be wary of, remember? What's changed, Jed? Why are you suddenly so sure he's no longer interested in you?"

"It'll all become clear in time." Smiling, Jed touched her arm. "Look across the marina to the town. D'you see the cathedral? Just in front of it is a hotel with a rooftop restaurant. They do wonderful food and you get a view over the rooftops of Malaga."

It sounded perfect, but she wasn't here to go sightseeing with Jed. "And Shona? What about her? We're supposed to spend today having our hair done and all that stuff. I want to see my bridesmaid dress and have a final try-on."

"You'll like it. I do. And don't worry, you'll look wonderful no matter what you do to your hair." He ruffled her hair.

"What aren't you telling me about Kenton? What is it between him and you?"

"Nothing, Rachel. I don't know the man, though I believe you've been out with him."

How had he found that out? Was Jed having her watched? "Spying on me now, are you? Yes, we did have dinner one night, but it was hardly a date. I don't like the man. He's far too cagey for me."

* * *

124

Kirsty Mallory was brought into the station that morning. She wasn't happy, and kept complaining that she'd done nothing wrong.

"It's Connor you need to talk to, not me," she said. "Him and Wignall had an arrangement. I was just the dogsbody."

"We gathered that," Jonny said. "But it was you who administered the drugs. We've seen the track marks on Wignall's lower legs. He couldn't have done that himself, and Connor wouldn't have had access to the home."

She lowered her gaze. "He knew the combination to get in."

"You gave it to him?"

"Look, I had no choice. Connor packs quite a punch when he's angry. He said he needed it and not to ask questions."

"How did Wignall pay for his fix? Connor would not have given him what he needed for nothing."

"Joe had money, a whole stash, and Connor knew about it. That's why he wanted the combination to get in. He planned to steal it one night when things were quiet."

"And did he?" Jonny asked.

"He didn't get the chance. Joe got killed and that was that."

"Where did Joe keep the money, Kirsty?"

"The bathroom cabinet has a false back. It's behind there."

"You should have told someone what was going on," Jonny said. "The manager, Mrs Wentworth, for example."

"I couldn't. Connor would have killed me, and anyway Wignall needed the stuff. He was an addict, as bad as Connor. He said if he didn't get what he needed, the consequences would be bad for me."

Elwyn took the photo of the three men from the file. "Do you know who these men are?"

Kirsty gave it a cursory glance. "No. It's just more of the rubbish Wignall took."

"Where is Connor this morning?" Jonny asked.

"He did one last night after you came round. He reckons you'll fit him up. Said he was scared and left."

"Do you know where he's gone?" Elwyn asked.

"No, and I haven't heard from him either. His mobile's switched off, so your guess is as good as mine. He doesn't tell me everything, you know. Connor has stuff going on all over. I don't want to get too involved. One of these days, he'll come unstuck."

"Is he afraid we'll get him for dealing drugs? He has form, so next time he'll go down. Or is it something or someone else?"

"It's what he does. Life gets tricky and Connor does one. He'll be back when things cool down. You lot can't prove anything anyway."

She had them there. Kirsty had just confessed to helping Wignall, but they still had nothing on Connor Young. There was a knock on the interview room door. It was Amy Metcalfe. She asked Elwyn for a word in the corridor.

"It looks like Sam Graham has turned up," she said.

Elwyn's relief was short-lived. "Is he here?"

"No, sir. If the body we've found is Graham, then he's dead."

CHAPTER TWENTY-THREE

Samuel Graham worked for Robert Knight, who owned a veterinary practice and ran an equine cremation service in Marple, a town on the other side of Stockport. Once the horrific discovery was made, the local force had attended, but on further investigation they had passed on the case to DCI King's team.

Jonny and Elwyn were now in the surgery with Knight. "See that car parked over there?" A young DC pointed it out to them. "It's been here all night. We checked the registration and it belongs to a Samuel Graham who works here in the practice. We checked the system and saw that he's listed as being a person of interest in your current case. Hence the call."

"You did the right thing," Elwyn said. "We've been looking for Graham."

Robert Knight was describing what they did. "We're a veterinary practice, specialising in larger animals, horses mostly. Ordinarily we do our best to fix them up when they're sick, but inevitably we do get some who have reached the end of their lives. Ten years ago, we extended the business to offer a cremation service for larger animals, horses in particular. We're one of very few in the country."

"And people want them cremating?" Jonny asked.

"Well, yes. You can hardly take a horse home and bury it in the garden. We cremate them and give the owner the ashes. We run the incinerator at night. Last night, Tom was doing his usual round and that's when he saw him." Knight nodded at the incinerator. "He panicked and rang me, and I contacted the local station."

Elwyn winced and turned aside. The machine was big enough to take a horse, so it was plenty big enough to accommodate the man whose burnt bones now occupied it.

"Tom shut down the incinerator at once, of course, but it had been running for some time, I'm afraid," Knight said. "When he realised it was a man in there, he went into shock. He's in that ambulance over there, still shaking."

"Did you know Sam Graham well?" Elwyn asked.

"He started with us a month ago. General stuff, nothing complicated — feeding the animals, mucking out, that sort of thing. He was good, he had an affinity with the animals. Are you sure that's Sam in there?"

He had a point. There was nothing left but bones. Finding a positive identity would be down to forensics — if that was even possible given the burning. "It's too early to tell. Can I have a list of your employees, please, as well as anyone else who was here yesterday and this morning?"

"What happens now?" Knight asked.

"Forensics will do their job and then we'll have the body removed. Until we've got everything we need, you'll have to keep the practice closed, I'm afraid," Elwyn said.

"But I've got operations scheduled for today."

"Sorry, sir, it can't be helped."

Dr Colin Butterworth was busy organising the removal of the body, with Jude in attendance.

"This one will be tricky," she told Elwyn. "We might get some material we can test for DNA, but I doubt it."

"Isn't there something about marrow in the long bones — the femur for example?" Elwyn asked.

"If there's any left. The intense heat might have done too much damage," she said.

"We'll know more in a day or two," Butterfield added. "We have a skeleton, that might tell us something."

"Grim," whispered Jonny. "I wonder if he knew what was happening to him?"

"God, I hope not," Elwyn said.

Jude took Elwyn aside. "Rachel is away, I believe?"

"She'll be back the day after tomorrow. Why? Do you want a word? I'm sure she won't mind if you ring her."

"What I have to say will unsettle her, so no. Come down to the lab this afternoon, I'd like a quiet chat."

* * *

"Our killer got to him when we couldn't," Jonny said on their way back to the station. "We should have protected him."

"We wasted too much time. But we did tell his mother. Rachel spelled out the danger. She got the distinct feeling that she knew perfectly well where he was," Elwyn said. "The woman should have told us. Anyway, we are getting ahead of ourselves. We don't even know that the victim is Graham."

"Oh it is, I feel it in my gut. Our killer's clever, he's one step ahead. What I don't understand is the different method. Burned not suffocated. Why do you think that was?" Jonny asked.

"From what we know of Graham, he was a big bloke. Perhaps the killer knew he'd give him a hard time. He'd not be a soft touch like Wignall and Alison Longhurst. We'll start going through that WhatsApp group, see if we can find a likely suspect," said Elwyn.

"We'll have to speak to Graham's mum," Jonny said. "Tell her what's happened, just in case."

Elwyn nodded. "We have no positive ID, so whatever we say at this point is conjecture. But you're right, we'll have to warn her. The chances are that the body is that of her son, but we'll tread carefully."

"Connor Young? Still want to find him?" Jonny asked.

"He is part of something else. Looking for him can wait. This case has to take priority. In my opinion, it's taken a back seat for long enough."

Elwyn was angry that they'd not found Graham in time. That was mostly down to Rachel's obsession with all things McAteer. Well, that would have to stop. They had three victims now, and Baslow was still missing. If he was still alive, the killer would be looking for him.

"Speak to your friend Hardacre again. Take Amy with you. Get him to open up, tell you about the other people who bought in to Woodsmoor. Ask if anyone stood out as being particularly vindictive — you know the stuff."

Elwyn was frustrated at having so little in the way of leads. The WhatsApp group numbered about twenty, it would take a while to trace and speak to each member. What they really needed was a bloody miracle.

CHAPTER TWENTY-FOUR

"I have some information for you," Jude told Elwyn. "I've prepared a report of my findings for DCI Kenton. I presume he'll pass them on, but in case he holds back, I'm telling you myself."

Elwyn had no idea what she was talking about, but he was curious.

"I was asked to look at two bodies discovered by a sheep farmer in the Staffordshire countryside. Both were buried in a shallow grave up in the moorland near the village of Longnor."

Elwyn was puzzled. That place was miles away and well outside their area. "What's that got to do with us? I know you're good, Jude, but why call on your services?"

"Because Kenton requested that I attend." She hesitated. "You see, the bodies belonged to Leonora Blake and Francis Baslow."

They sat in silence for a while as Elwyn took this in — and tried to work it out. He could understand Kenton's interest in Blake, but why had she been found with Baslow? What was the connection between them? "I don't understand," he said eventually. "There's no way they could have known each other."

"We've found nothing to prove that they did. But they both had bullet wounds to the head. Bullets from the same handgun, Elwyn. You're the detective, but to me that suggests the same killer."

"And there's no doubt about their identities?"

"Leonora was buried with her belongs, notably her phone, and DNA confirmed that the other body was Baslow. We're still processing the DNA on Blake's body. As far as I'm concerned, there is no doubt. The killer or killers obviously never expected them to be found."

Elwyn had a bad feeling. Now, why was that? Did the killers imagine they were immune from the law? "Were they killed at the same time?"

"No. Leonora Blake's body is in a more advanced state of decomposition than that of Baslow."

"And Kenton has the report?" he asked.

"Yes. I emailed it to him first thing. I'm surprised he hasn't told you. Given your current case, you need to know."

"Leonora Blake was part of the trafficking gang. Baslow was not. The only thing they had in common was Joseph Wignall. He was part of that gang too, and he took Baslow's place in the nursing home. Whoever killed him can't have realised he had the wrong man."

"Quite a conundrum," said Jude. "I don't envy you your job, Elwyn."

He rubbed his head. "What about the body that was brought in earlier?"

"We're still cleaning him up, but I did look at the skull. There is a depression in the skull that I'd say is consistent with blunt instrument trauma," Jude said.

"Male?"

"Ask me in a couple of days when we've finished the cleaning and pieced the skeleton together. We've still got a heap of measurements and tests to carry out. There should be more results soon. I'll ring you."

"What we need, Jude, is confirmation that he's Graham."

"All in good time, Elwyn. We're doing our best. But it looks highly likely. The body fits the description we have of Graham, and the man is still missing."

So, Wignall and Longhurst were not an inside job. The deaths of Graham and Baslow confirmed that.

There was nothing he could do here, so Elwyn made his way back to the station. The hope now was that the killer was one of Woodsmoor's disgruntled customers, and that he or she was part of the WhatsApp group Jonny was investigating. He was tempted to give Rachel a call and bring her up to date, but he resisted. It wouldn't be fair. She deserved all the time off she could get.

From his car, he rang the incident room and spoke to Jonny. "I'm going to call on Sam Graham's mother, give her the heads-up. She may be able to tell me something useful. I'll be back shortly."

"Kenton's been in. He's asking for you," Jonny said.

That'd be about the report from Jude. "I'll speak to him when I return. If he asks again, tell him where I've gone."

* * *

Graham's mother wasn't happy to see the police on her doorstep a second time. She let him in reluctantly. "I have to go out soon," she said. She seemed on edge.

"Mrs Graham, was your son working at Knight's veterinary practice in Marple?"

Her face fell. "How did you find out? He wanted to keep his head down for a few weeks. He told me that someone was after him."

"So he was there?"

She looked away and nodded. "It wasn't to be for long. He told me he'd be back by the end of the month."

"This person who was after him — did he tell you who it was?"

She evaded the question. "Sam didn't always do manual work, you know. He used to have a good, well-paid

133

job selling property. But the company went bust, leaving a number of their customers very angry. People had paid over good money, thousands in some instances, and got nothing in return. He wasn't proud of what he'd done but he didn't have the money to put it right. He told me that one of those customers had sworn to get even — he'd lost his life savings to the company. Sam wasn't too concerned at first but then that man was killed in the home, and Alison was killed too. I met her a couple of times, she was nice. Sam told me he was terrified that it'd be him next."

She was visibly upset, staring at him, no doubt with a dozen questions she wanted to ask but not wanting to hear his answers.

"This morning, a body was found on the vet's premises. We think it might be your son."

Through her tears, she said, "Do you want me to identify Sam?"

How to tell her? "It's not that simple, I'm afraid. There was a fire." He didn't want to tell her the horrendous truth yet. There was a very slim chance it might not be Graham. "The body was burned. It wouldn't be advisable to see him."

"It isn't fair. He had such a hard time of it recently. I desperately wanted him to be happy, but he had no luck. After he lost Nina, he thought the fates had done their worst, and then this happens."

"Nina?" Elwyn asked.

"The love of his life, a beautiful girl. They got engaged last Christmas and should have been married by now."

"She left him?"

"Nina took her own life a few months ago. After that, Sam didn't care about anything anymore."

CHAPTER TWENTY-FIVE

"Kenton is on the prowl, sir," Jonny told Elwyn when he returned. "He must have been in here four times in the last hour, asking for you. Is there something we should know?"

"I'm not sure," Elwyn replied. He didn't say anything about the Staffordshire bodies — they belonged to a different case, the one Kenton was investigating. Better go and speak to him.

It was odd seeing Kenton where Harding used to sit. The super's office had changed too. It was considerably tidier, the files all neatly stacked and the desk clear.

"Dr Glover has emailed me a report. She's told you about her findings, I believe," Kenton said.

Elwyn nodded. "The discovery impacts our current case, sir. We have been looking for Francis Baslow. In fact, we did wonder if he was complicit in the murders."

"Continue with your investigations but drop any further reference to Baslow, where he was found and who with. It was down to chance, and has no bearing on your case."

"With respect, sir, I think it does. We believe Baslow was mistaken for a man called Joseph Wignall. Wignall and Baslow met in hospital and swapped places when they left. I can only presume that the swap suited them both, although

I doubt they were honest about their reasons. It might help our current case to know who took and killed Baslow."

"It wouldn't, take my word for it. Have you heard from DCI King?" he said abruptly.

"No, sir."

"If you do speak to her, don't mention the Staffordshire bodies. Leave it until she returns."

"Fair enough," Elwyn said. "I wouldn't want to burden her anyway."

"Good, and don't inform the rest of your team either for the time being."

It was important information, so why was Kenton being so secretive? Until this moment, Elwyn had questioned Rachel's mistrust of the DCI but now he was having doubts himself. "We thought Leonora Blake was in the witness protection programme," he said.

"She was, and that's why I want this keeping quiet for now. Someone leaked her whereabouts, which gives me a problem because I can count on the fingers of one hand the number of people who knew where she was."

"Whoever was responsible, it wasn't one of our team," Elwyn said. "And I will have to give them some explanation for why we're no longer looking for Baslow."

"Make something up," Kenton said dismissively. "And you're wrong. A member of this team did know where Leonora was."

Elwyn walked back to the office, pondering on who that might be. Surely Kenton wasn't pointing the finger at Rachel? She may have known, and she was a high-ranking officer. Kenton's orders or not, he'd have a word as soon as she got back.

"I wouldn't mind another chat with Cyril Hardacre," Elwyn said to Jonny when he got to the incident room. "There are still a couple of things we should clear up." He turned to Amy. "You carry on with what you were doing. Jonny and I won't be long."

"What do you want to know?" Jonny asked, reaching for his jacket.

"In his statement he said Woodsmoor's people arranged the conveyancing. They were using their own people. I'm wondering if the customers received any paperwork from the solicitors, letters and so on. If so, we should talk to them."

They were just leaving the office when Amy called to them. "The data from Wignall's laptop is in. There's not much on it, just a load of photographs. What d'you want them to do?"

"Tell them I'll come and have a look when we get back." He and Jonny made their way down the stairs.

"He must have spent his life snapping away," Jonny said.

That got Elwyn thinking. Wignall travelled across Europe for the traffickers. It was likely he took photos of what he saw. Were there any more of the man Rachel had shown him? Perhaps that was why he'd hidden the laptop.

* * *

Cyril Hardacre invited them in. "I've spoken to one or two of the lads since your last visit. We wouldn't know where to start if we wanted revenge, but Larry might. He swore he'd get even. He said he would hire a private investigator to find those involved with Woodsmoor."

"Larry?" Elwyn asked.

"Larry McGuire, a builder. He has offices in Ardwick."

Jonny wrote down the name in his notebook. "Do you recall which solicitors were dealing with the legal stuff?"

"We never got that far," Cyril admitted. "An agreement was promised, searches on the land, the lot, but it never happened. That Longhurst woman said that if we didn't want to miss out, we had to move quick, just pay over the money and worry about the paperwork later. She assured me and the wife that there was no problem, it would follow in a matter of days. Of course, it never did."

"Do you know where we can find Larry McGuire?" asked Elwyn.

"Here's his card. That's his office address in Ardwick."

"Was there anyone else who wanted to get revenge on the people from Woodsmoor? Anything you picked up on?" asked Elwyn.

"We all did a lot of bellyaching, couldn't get over what had happened and how stupid we'd been, but for most of us that's all it was. Where Larry was concerned, it'd been his wife who'd got conned. She'd intended it to be a sixtieth birthday present for him. Some present — practically broke the bank. She'd ordered the biggest bungalow and a shed load of extras. Stupid woman must have parted with a fortune. Larry took it bad. He's got a temper too. I once saw him knock seven bells out of some scally at the golf club for scratching his car."

"Thank you, you've been very helpful," Elwyn said. They stood up. "If anything else occurs to you, here's my card."

Back in the car, Jonny asked him what he thought.

"Get onto Amy, ask her to look at what conversations Larry McGuire was party to in that group. Anything inflammatory, get her to text me. In the meantime, we'll go and have a word with the man."

* * *

The builder's yard was large, and from the amount of stock on sale and the three large vans parked in the bays with the McGuire name plastered across the sides, obviously successful. A sign at the entrance advertised the range of building work the company undertook.

"They've been here donkey's years," Jonny said. "I think my dad knows the current owner. They're members of the same club."

"McGuire must be a pretty shrewd operator to have made such a success of this little lot. Why would he fall for a scam like Woodsmoor?" They went into the office.

"Can I help?" asked the receptionist.

Elwyn showed her his badge. "We'd like a word with Mr McGuire."

"I'll get him, he's just across the yard."

"He's got a lot to lose," Jonny said. "Somehow I can't see someone that owns all this being a killer."

"We'll reserve judgement until we've spoken to him," Elwyn said.

The man who came to meet them was tall and thickset with grey hair. Obviously a hands-on businessman, he was wearing overalls.

"I'm McGuire. What can I do for you?"

"I believe you bought into the Woodsmoor scheme. Is that right?" Elwyn said.

McGuire grimaced. "My wife did, not me. If I'd known what she was doing, I'd have stopped her straight away. Worst thing she ever did. Took us for a small fortune them bloody robbing gits did. Moira was completely taken in. They waved a glossy brochure in front of her face and that was that. Found them rogues, have you? Is that what you've come to tell me?"

"Not exactly." Elwyn coughed. "The three directors of Woodsmoor have been murdered."

McGuire smiled. "Best bit of news I've heard all year. Got what they deserved, and I'm not sorry I said it."

"You're pretty cut up about being ripped off. That's understandable. We've been told that a few months ago you were raging, that you didn't hold back on how you'd like to get even," Jonny said.

"Okay, I was angry — raging like you said," McGuire admitted, "but it didn't last long. I blew off a bit of steam, we all did, but I didn't kill anyone. I wouldn't know where to start."

"If we give you a couple of dates, can you tell us where you were?"

McGuire gave Elwyn a filthy look. "Go on then."

Elwyn took out his notebook and gave him the dates when Wignall and Longhurst had been murdered.

"That's simple enough, mate. I was languishing in North Manchester General having a hernia fixed. Check it out. They'll back me up."

CHAPTER TWENTY-SIX

"We've been working on this case for days and we're still no closer," Elwyn complained.

They were on their way back to the station, with Jonny driving. "Want to take a look at that laptop when we get back?"

"It belonged to Wignall and he's a different case. I don't see what looking at a load of his old photographs will give us."

"Desperate measures, sir."

"We've missed something, must have," Elwyn said. "It wasn't an inside job — everyone involved in the Woodsmoor venture is dead — so it has to be down to one of the customers. And don't forget the confetti and finger taking either. That has to be significant."

"It's a long shot, but I'll have another look at the WhatsApp list we've got. There may be someone on it who was planning to get wed. He loses all his money and the killings were his way of exacting revenge," Jonny said.

Elwyn shrugged. "Or it's a complete red herring and has nothing to do with it."

"It means something, I know it does," Jonny said.

"The person who lost the most was McGuire, and he was the angriest too. Check his alibi anyway. It's a long shot but he might have lied."

When they got back, Amy had just put the phone down. "That was Jude Glover," she said to Elwyn. "Says she has something interesting and wants you to get down there."

It was getting late and Elwyn had a thumping headache. All he wanted was to get back to his sister's place and put his feet up. "I'll ring her back, tell her I'll go in the morning. I've had it for today." He pointed to the clock. "Why don't you two call it a day too?"

Amy didn't need telling twice. Before Elwyn could blink she was halfway out the door.

Jonny was checking the messages left on his desk. "The CCTV is finally in from the hospital. I'll stay and have a look at it, and Wignall's laptop. If I find anything, I'll ring you, sir."

* * *

In Jonny's opinion this was the best time of the day. A quiet, empty office and he was left alone to follow his instincts. He'd been down to see the techies and retrieved the laptop. He had a printout of the data found, but he wanted to examine the thing himself. Wignall was part of the trafficking investigation but the two cases overlapped. Wignall had hidden the laptop, therefore there had to be something important on it. Jonny was ambitious. It would do him no harm to find something Kenton could use.

There were a couple of emails, both advertising photography equipment. He dismissed them. Wignall's photos would take days to plough through. He had driven all the way across Europe, and it seemed he'd taken a photo at every opportunity. Jonny scrolled through them quickly. As far as he could make out, there was nothing of particular interest. He yawned. Perhaps this wasn't such a good idea after all. He'd look at the internet search history next and then he'd call it a day.

It seemed Joseph Wignall had spent a great deal of time researching a firm called GoldStar Logistics. It wasn't a company Jonny had heard of before. They had a website but weren't listed at Companies House. Wignall had visited the site several times a day, he had to have been looking for something, or someone. But the website gave little away, it didn't mention who owned the company and gave only a brief description of how they operated.

Back to the photos. Jonny's head was spinning and his eyes hurt. As far as he could see, there was nothing on the laptop that would help. But then why had Wignall hidden the thing?

He pushed it to one side and logged on to his own computer. He'd take a look at that CCTV from the hospital before he went home. The note on his desk said they'd done their best to narrow it down as finely as they could. Another yawn. He hoped he wasn't going to be here all night.

The footage was a good five minutes in before the two men appeared. Baslow was on foot, Wignall in a wheelchair. A porter wheeled Wignall through the rotating doors and went back inside. Minutes later, a Bolton's taxi turned up and Wignall was helped into it. No surprises so far. Baslow waited another few minutes until a second car pulled up beside him. Jonny leaned forward, watching closely. The car wasn't a taxi, it was a small hatchback. He strained to see the man alighting from the driver's side. Surprise, surprise. It was Connor Young. The driver from Bolton's had been right. That lad was up to his neck in this. They had to find him and bring him in.

Despite the late hour, he decided to give Elwyn a call.

"For heaven's sake, Jonny! You woke me up. I was spark out on the sofa."

"Sorry, but I wanted to give you the heads-up. I found nothing on Wignall's laptop, but the hospital CCTV was fruitful. Bolton's picked up Wignall like we were told, and it was Connor Young who picked up Baslow."

"Good work, Jonny. I'll let you off for waking me up. Young needs finding and bringing in. He will have to tell us where he took Baslow and how he knew him."

"Kirsty Mallory got bail. Want me to call at hers on my way home?"

"No, it's late. I'll meet you there at about eight in the morning."

That was fine with Jonny. He didn't fancy arguing the toss with Kirsty, while he was knackered after a long day. He picked up his mobile and rang his dad.

"They're keeping me a couple of days longer," Bobby Farrell said. "But I'm getting there. I feel more like my old self."

"Sorry I can't visit tonight — the case is proving difficult and time consuming. I've been stuck in the office for most of the evening." It struck Jonny that his dad might have heard of GoldStar, the organisation that had interested Wignall so much. Bobby Farrell imported sportswear and goods from all over the world and he mixed with the business fraternity.

"GoldStar? I know they're fake, set up as some sort of tax dodge. My advice is to give them a wide swerve. Believe me, son, you do not want to get involved with that lot."

Jonny knew that tone. His dad was holding back. "You know who runs it, don't you?"

"I don't want you in their sights, Jonny. They're a bad lot."

"Look, Dad, it's my job to get involved. This could be important, you know. We're working on a murder case. I can't afford to miss anything. What aren't you telling me?"

"I don't know anything specific, only that the person behind GoldStar is a villain of the first order."

"Name, Dad."

"I tell you and you'll go haring off for a chat. Do that, son, and within days you'll disappear. I'm not taking that risk."

"No one is above the law," Jonny said.

"This bastard is, believe me."

CHAPTER TWENTY-SEVEN

Day Seven

Having been charged with handling and selling drugs, Kirsty Mallory was out on bail awaiting further action. She answered the door in her dressing gown and stared at the two detectives with bleary eyes. "It's too bloody early for this shit." She yawned. "What d'you want anyway?"

Elwyn got straight to the point. "Connor Young. Where is he?"

"He's not here, so do one, copper." She nodded at Jonny. "I haven't seen him since *he* came round."

"Guilty conscience," Jonny said.

"He's done nowt. Not that you'll believe him."

"Forget the drugs for the time being, Young picked up the real Francis Baslow from the hospital. We'd like to know what he did with him."

Kirsty shook her head. "That doesn't sound right. Why would he do that? He never said owt to me."

Elwyn had to admit that the girl did look genuinely puzzled. "You're sure he didn't make any smart comments about a lift he'd given someone? He must have known Baslow, or at least what he looked like, to pick him up like that."

"Joe will have put him in touch."

Plausible, but no help. "You're sure Connor didn't say where he'd been that day?"

"How am I supposed to remember that? It were months ago. Get real, copper, I can barely remember what happened yesterday."

"If he comes back here, you must contact us, Kirsty. This is a murder investigation and you don't want to get yourself into any more trouble than you are already."

"Look, I can tell you this much. Connor's been afraid of his own shadow lately. He was convinced someone were following him. Having you lot on his tail were the final straw. He'll be hiding somewhere. Like I said, he'll surface when he's ready."

"When he does, we want to know," Jonny said. "And don't you go doing a disappearing act either."

They had just turned to go when Elwyn's mobile rang. It was Jude Glover.

"I need a word," she began. "We've had something of a breakthrough with our unknown and it might help you prove his identity."

"We'll be right there." He turned to Jonny. "Jude's found something. She wants us down there."

"I'll drive," Jonny said, unlocking the car. "By the way, have you heard of a firm called GoldStar?"

"Where did you get that name from?" Elwyn asked. GoldStar was the operation Rachel had asked him about, but where had Jonny heard it?

"I had a look at Wignall's laptop last night. They're a haulage company so it seems. He kept visiting their website and I don't understand why. There's nothing much on it."

"They're a new one to me," Elwyn lied. For the time being he'd keep what little he knew to himself, until he'd spoken to Rachel.

"My dad knows a lot of people in the Manchester business community so I asked him. He warned me off, and I mean seriously. Told me not to get involved, reckons they're dangerous. He even went as far as saying some big-time villain ran the show."

"Did he give you the name?"

"No, he refused. He doesn't want me trying to find the guy, whoever he is."

Big-time villain, Elwyn thought. A name connected to the Blake case. That could be Jed McAteer.

* * *

The skeleton was laid out on a table in the lab. Jude and her crew had done what they could. What was left of the bones had been cleaned up and assembled.

"Male, tall, and I can confirm that he was struck on the back of the head." She picked up the skull and held it out for them to look at. "See here at the back, there's an indentation," Jude said. "A single blow with something heavy."

Jonny winced. There was no way he'd be able to do her job. "He was dead then — before the cremation?"

"We can't know that for sure," Jude said, "but after a blow like that he'd certainly be unconscious."

Elwyn was staring at the right leg. "I realise the bones had a hard time in the fire, but why is this one in pieces?"

Jude smiled. "Ah, this is the bit that might help you. At some time in the past this man had a knee replacement fitted. See the metal pieces here?" She picked one up. "They are fitted above and below the knee joint. The replacement kneecap will have been made of a plastic so burned to nothing, but the metal parts remained. I've requested his notes from the local GP practice, but it might hurry things up if you ask Graham's mother whether he'd had this type of surgery. If she says yes, then it's one step nearer to identifying him."

CHAPTER TWENTY-EIGHT

They got back into the car. "Where to next?" Jonny asked.

"We'll go and have a look at that bathroom of Wignall's at Hawthorne Lodge. See if the money is still there, if it ever was," Elwyn said.

Jonny was concentrated on his mobile. "Kirsty isn't stupid. She'll know it's easily checked. Shouldn't we have a word with Graham's mother first?"

"All in good time. What are you up to?"

"Searching for that website — GoldStar. Yep. It's still there and still as useless. There's no contact details and not even a hint of what they do. It's literally just a page with images of container lorries. Why go to the expense, if the entire thing is fake anyway?"

"What did your dad say?" Elwyn asked.

"That the company was set up as some sort of tax dodge, but there'll be more to it. I wish he'd talk to me, stop treating me like a six-year-old and understand that I've a job to do."

"He's just being protective," Elwyn said.

His mobile rang — Amy.

She sounded excited. "Something of a breakthrough, sir. Pat Wentworth was a member of that WhatsApp group. That means she must have been a Woodsmoor customer."

"Good work, Amy. We're on our way there now to check something else, I'll speak to her, see what she knows."

"Something happened?" Jonny asked as he pulled up outside Hawthorne Lodge.

"What d'you reckon to the manager, Pat Wentworth? Is she on the level? Or could she have been the one who fed Wignall the drugs?"

"Why d'you ask? She's not been in the frame before," Jonny said.

"Well, she is now. Amy's found her name in that WhatsApp group. She must have been a customer of Woodsmoor, and that made the man she thought was Baslow a sitting target. What d'you think?" Emlyn sounded excited.

Jonny wasn't sure. "The drugs thing is more likely to be Kirsty. The girl's got form, and she was his carer. He'd be more likely to approach her than Wentworth."

"I'm also wondering why Wignall ended up in Hawthorne. I know it's cheap, but there are cheaper ones, nearer to his sister. Supposing Pat Wentworth wangled that too?"

"Well, she isn't comfortable having us around, I know that much," Jonny said.

Pat Wentworth prickled at the sight of the two detectives. "You've spoken to the residents, upset my staff — what else do you want?" she said.

Elwyn would take this slowly, dealing with the money first. "We believe Joseph Wignall had money stashed away in his room," he said. "Would you mind if we took a look?"

They didn't have a warrant, so if she refused, it would cause a delay. They were relying on her goodwill.

"We're expecting a new resident to occupy it before the end of the week. The room has been cleaned from top to bottom and we've found nothing."

"We know exactly where to look," Jonny said. "It'll only take a few minutes."

"Don't upset anyone. Winnie has been very unsettled since your visit," she said.

As soon as they were in the room, Jonny went straight to the bathroom to check the cabinet. Elwyn remained with Pat Wentworth.

"When the man you thought was Baslow came here, did you know who he was?" he asked.

"How could I? I'd never met the man before."

"But you knew the name. You must have seen it on the paperwork you received from Woodsmoor. Baslow was one of the directors."

Pat Wentworth gave him a poisonous look. "The man was a thief and a crook," she spat. "Him and his cohorts swindled thousands out of people who trusted him. It wasn't fair. He was never going to be punished."

"So you decided to take the law into your own hands?" Elwyn asked.

"It wasn't like that. I did nothing to harm him."

"But you didn't stop someone else having a go," said Elwyn. "You turned a blind eye to the drugs Kirsty was feeding him, and then there's the code for the main entrance."

Just then, Jonny reappeared with a wad of cash in his hand. "Exactly where Kirsty said it would be, sir." He smiled. "There must be at least a grand here."

"I'm afraid you'll have to come to the station with us, Mrs Wentworth. We need a proper word," Emlyn said.

She didn't look happy. Her eyes hardly left the bundle of cash which Jonny was transferring to an evidence bag. "I'd no idea he had that much hidden away. Kirsty should have told me."

* * *

Back at the station, Elwyn decided to interview Pat Wentworth with Amy. Amy now had a full list of names from the WhatsApp group, and Wentworth might be able to shed some light on who they were and how they reacted when they realised they'd been cheated.

"Tell me about the meeting of Woodsmoor customers you went to," he began.

"There were two meetings, both in a pub called the 'Mitre' in central Manchester. The first one got very heated." She looked from one detective to the other. "You have to understand that people had lost a lot of money — in some cases everything they'd saved. To say they were angry was an understatement."

"Was there anyone in particular who spoke out about getting even, or harming any of the Woodsmoor directors?" Emlyn asked.

"Larry McGuire certainly wasn't happy. He's a successful businessman and he likes to throw his weight about. His wife had bought in and he swore he'd find the Woodsmoor people and make them give back every penny they'd taken."

They'd already spoken to McGuire, and his alibi checked out. "Anyone else?" asked Elwyn.

"Most of the group were retired, and frankly too old to do much about what had happened. They bellyached a lot, but that was as far as it was ever going to go. I did worry about Ian, though. He was younger, angry like everyone else, but he kept it in, internalised it like some people do. I did wonder if he might do something."

"Did he talk about getting even?" Amy asked.

"He said very little, just sat in a corner and seethed. I tried talking to him but he was a closed book."

"His full name?" asked Elwyn.

"Ian Johnson. He lives in Longsight somewhere."

"You knew Baslow was one of the Woodsmoor crew. Did you tell anyone in the group that he was in your home?"

"No. I promise I didn't. I was worried about repercussions, but," she paused dropping her gaze, "someone knew. A week before he was killed, a note came through the door — four digits. It said I should change the entry code to that."

"And that's what you did? That's how the killer gained access to the building?"

"Yes. But not straight away. I thought if I delayed, then whoever was doing this might get fed up. But he didn't, instead the threats came thick and fast. He threatened to burn the place down, it was then I changed the code. But I didn't know Baslow was going to be killed."

"Were the threats made by note too?"

"Yes."

"Do you still have them?" asked Amy.

"No, I burned the lot. I knew it had to have something to do with Baslow."

"You didn't have to do what it said. You could have come to us when you got the note."

Pat Wentworth flushed. "Why should I? That man deserved everything he got. People were left without any hope of getting their money back."

"But it wasn't Baslow who was killed, was it?" Elwyn said. "And what about the other two directors? They've been murdered too."

CHAPTER TWENTY-NINE

Elwyn went through the list of names again. "We've spoken to a couple of these and we've interviewed Pat Wentworth. The Ian Johnson she mentioned is worth a chat." He looked at Jonny. "Before we start on the rest of the list, you and Amy go and find him, see if he has an alibi for the times of the murders."

"Dr Glover rang. She wants a word," Stella said, handing him a note.

Elwyn had assumed she had some proof that their skeleton was Sam Graham, but the note was about the death of Alison Longhurst.

"This looks important. I'm off to see Jude. We'll catch up later."

Kenton collared him on his way out. "How's the case going? Found your killer yet?"

"We're getting there, sir."

"It's been a while now. I expect results, so pull out all the stops. Three bodies, Elwyn, and no one in the frame. It's not good enough."

Cheeky bastard. The team were working flat out, and given the complexity of the case, they were lucky to have got this far.

* * *

Jude Glover greeted him with a smile. "I've got some results for you," she said. "Something you weren't expecting."

"Sam Graham?" Elwyn asked.

"All in good time, these things can't be rushed, you know."

"I could do with positive proof. I've left his poor mother in limbo, not knowing if her son is dead or not."

Ignoring his words, Jude said, "My news is about Alison Longhurst. As we know, she was suffocated. Remember the blue fibres we found in her mouth that we thought must come from a cushion."

Elwyn nodded. "With you so far."

"Well, we've found the cushion. There is no doubt — it has traces of her saliva on it."

Elwyn was puzzled. "Was it in her place after all?"

Jude shook her head. "No. We found it in Joseph Wignall's house. As you asked, we did a sweep for prints and the like. Well, while we were there, a sharp-eyed technician spotted it. It was brought in, and tested positive for Longhurst's DNA. Also, the fibres that make up the cushion are a match for those found on the body."

Elwyn tried to make sense of what Jude had just told him. At the very least, it amounted to another connection between Wignall and the Woodsmoor case. "We found evidence that someone had been staying in Wignall's place — the sleeping bag and discarded food packages. Can you help identify who that might have been?"

"We're working on it," Jude said. "We've retrieved a half-eaten sandwich and some dishes from the sink, which might yield DNA. Even better, we found blood spatters in the bathroom sink. Not much, the sort that might be left if a man cut himself shaving. I'm confident they will give us what we need."

"Thanks, Jude, you're a real wonder. We can now work on the premise that whoever was staying in Wignall's house is our killer."

Jude smiled. "Naturally, when we have a DNA profile, we'll run it through the system to see if there's a match. When we have something positive, you'll be the first to know."

* * *

Ian Johnson lived alone on a small estate of new houses in Longsight.

Jonny introduced his colleagues. "Mr Johnson? DC Farrell and DC Metcalfe from East Manchester CID. Can we ask you a few questions?"

He fiddled nervously with his glasses, pushing them up his long nose. "If you could make it quick. I'm not very well today."

"Can we come in?" Amy asked.

He looked back along the hallway. "It depends on what you want."

He was acting very edgy. Jonny got straight to the point. "We're here about Woodsmoor, Mr Johnson. You bought in and lost a lot of money. Want to tell us about it?"

"Not really. I don't like talking about it, it makes me upset. And I'd rather my sister didn't find out." He gave another glance back inside. "Ask someone else. I wasn't the only one that was cheated, there were a number of us. Is that why you're here, have you recovered it?"

"No," Amy said. "We're investigating the murders of the three Woodsmoor directors."

Johnson took a step back. He looked utterly terrified. "It has nothing to do with me. I've done nothing wrong. You can't prove anything against me."

"We're not accusing you, Mr Johnson, we'd just like your take on what happened," Jonny said.

"We were scammed, they stole our money. I was very upset. They were bad people. Like the others, I lost thousands. I really wanted that bungalow." His voice shook. "It would have been nice to live in the countryside and have all those amenities. I fish, you know."

"Have you met up with any of the other buyers recently?" Jonny asked.

"No. I have nothing in common with them. I went to the meetings, but we were never going to get anywhere. They were a rabble — shouting and swearing. It wasn't very pleasant. You should ask them about the murders, not me."

"But you were angry, Mr Johnson. Mrs Wentworth was worried about how the sorry business had affected you."

"Pat's a nice lady, I liked her. But she's got it wrong. I was upset at first, but I've come to terms with it now."

Ian Johnson was a slightly built man and not very tall. He might have managed to deal with Wignall and Alison Longhurst, but he would not have fared well against Sam Graham, who was reputedly a big bloke. They were wasting time here.

Soon they were back in the car. "Weirdo," Amy said. "He gave me the creeps. What about you?"

"I doubt he's our man. If you want my opinion, he's physically not up to it."

* * *

"Jude hopes to have DNA from the killer very soon," Elwyn said. "She'll run it through the database and see if there's a match." Jonny and Amy were back at the station.

"If it was one of the WhatsApp group there's not much chance of that, unless one of them has a record."

Jonny had a point. "Well, we'll DNA test the whole lot of them if we have to. We've eliminated everyone else. Our killer has to be in there somewhere," Elwyn said.

"How long?" asked Amy.

"Tomorrow, with luck, she'll ring me."

"We could start collecting samples from the group, just in case," Amy suggested. "We could get uniform on it."

"Okay," Elwyn said. "Get it organised."

CHAPTER THIRTY

It was over. All that was left now was to sort the money. Everyone believed that Baslow had stolen it, cleared out the Woodsmoor account and absconded, leaving no trace. And no one had questioned it. It fitted with the image of the wicked scammer who'd defrauded the gullible out of their savings, forcing people who couldn't afford it to take out loans they'd never be able to pay back. He smiled. All he needed now was a plane ticket out of the country. Effectively, he was free, clear, and very wealthy. He could think of nothing that could go wrong. As far as he was concerned, his planning had been perfect.

But there were always doubts. He'd never been a confident person, and this was too important to foul up. He went over every detail in his head one more time. Had he forgotten anything that would lead the police to him? No. He was worrying unnecessarily. This time, he'd won the game.

* * *

Jude called with the bad news. "We have a DNA profile from Wignall's house and there's no match on the database."

Elwyn sighed. "There's a number of people who bought into Woodsmoor and lost their money. They met up, vented their anger and discussed how to move forward. They formed an online group — as far as we know, all of them were members. We've taken samples from every one of them, with luck you'll find a match there."

"I bet we don't," Jude said.

This took Elwyn aback. "Why not?"

"Think about it. He is an unknown, and he's well aware of it. You won't find him by searching the database, we'll need samples to test against. His big mistake was leaving his DNA all over Wignall's house, including his blood and the cushion he killed Alison Longhurst with. He will have known that terrace was scheduled for demolition. I bet he didn't expect anything to be found. He didn't know about Wignall, he thought he'd killed Baslow. Even so, he's not on the database and I bet he's not in that group either."

All Elwyn's elation disappeared. He didn't want to admit it, but Jude had a point. "That group is our last hope, Jude. If we don't find him there, we're lost."

"Have you heard from Rachel?" Jude asked.

"No, I don't want to update her about the case, or that we found Baslow's body. She's on holiday. Plenty of time for all that when she gets back," Elwyn said.

Jude grunted. "She won't thank you."

Elwyn knew that, but Rachel deserved some down time and she wouldn't get any if her head was full of the case. "How're you doing with him?" He nodded at the covered skeleton on a table.

"Not very well. Sam Graham wasn't registered with any of the local GPs. He must have been one healthy individual. I'm checking the hospitals in an effort to find which one did his knee. Have you spoken to his mother yet?"

Elwyn shook his head. "Next on my list."

"Get the samples from the group to me quick and I'll turn them round as fast as I can. But don't hold your breath."

Jude seemed very sure of it, and Elwyn had a horrible feeling she was right. The problem was, they'd exhausted all the suspects. It was not an inside job, and if the samples proved that it wasn't one of the people who'd bought into Woodsmoor, what then? He couldn't recall any other case that had given them such problems.

* * *

Back to Hyde to speak to Sam Graham's mother. Elwyn had got Stella to ring ahead to tell her he was coming.

"Have you found my Sam yet?" she said on opening the door. "There has to be some mistake, I don't believe he's dead, I'm his mother. I'd feel it. I read in the papers about that body they found in Marple. It can't be Sam. I can't think of anyone who'd do that to him."

He smiled at her. "The forensic people are still doing tests, Mrs Graham. And I hope you're right, and Sam is safe. We could certainly do with having a word with him. I came here to ask you something."

"I'll do anything to help," she said. "I just want him found safe and well."

"Did Sam ever have surgery on one of his knees?"

She shook her head. "Not his knee, it was his right arm — he broke it playing rugger. Nasty break it was too, he had to have it pinned."

"You're sure he never had problems with his right knee?"

"Certain. I'm his mother, I'd know if he'd had an operation like that."

Now what? Elwyn's head was in a spin when he left the house. He sat in his car, trying to make sense of the new information. Could Jude have got it wrong? It was unlikely, but he rang her anyway.

"I've spoken to Sam Graham's mother. She says he never had knee surgery but he did break his arm and had to have it pinned. Is there any way . . . ?"

Jude laughed. "Elwyn Pryce! Don't you dare even ask. You are actually suggesting that I don't know the difference between a leg and an arm!"

"Er . . . no, Jude, but I'm confused. The woman was so certain."

"Well, take it from me, this skeleton never had a broken arm but did have a knee replacement."

Elwyn groaned. "In that case our skeleton is not Sam Graham. We found his car up at Knight's. Would you have it swept for prints and so on, Jude? We might get something from it."

CHAPTER THIRTY-ONE

"Shona looks gorgeous, this is one of the best weekends ever," Rachel said wistfully. "The ceremony was so romantic, it's obvious that Juan loves her very much. When I married Alan, it was a rush job, I was four months gone and we didn't have a lot of money."

Jed kissed her cheek. "You always look gorgeous. You're the prettiest bridesmaid here."

She punched his arm. "I'm the only bridesmaid here, flatterer. They'll be leaving soon." She nodded at the happy pair. "Shona and me have hardly spoken. What with you demanding all my attention, there's been no time, and I really wanted a good catch-up."

"Well, you've caught up with me instead."

"You don't count. Shona's my friend."

"Bloody cheek. What am I then?"

"A damn nuisance most of the time. These days I seem to spend my life praying that you are not at the bottom of every case I investigate."

Jed McAteer steered Rachel away from the bridal group. "I'm not, I promise you. I gave all that up years ago, as well you know. I shouldn't have to convince you — my new reputation speaks for itself. These days, I'm a developer. I build things. I work well within the law and I don't intend to change that."

Rachel looked up into his dark eyes. She wanted to believe him. The last two days had been the happiest she'd spent in years. Jed was still the love of her life, and this time with him had been precious. "You've no idea how much I want to trust you, Jed, but I can't. You're a wanted man, there's no getting away from that. You could be picked up at any time."

"I expected more from you, Rachel." He turned his back on her and returned to the rest of the group. Rachel knew she'd soured the mood. Jed was getting tired of trying to convince her.

"Photos, Rachel!" Shona called out to her. "A final one with you and Juan and then we're out of here." She put her arm around her friend's waist. "The light has gone out of your eyes, Rachel," she whispered. "Please don't fight with him, life's too short."

Rachel wished things were that simple. "I love him, but we can't be together. He's wanted in the UK and the law won't let up."

Shona hugged Rachel close. "Then stay here. Have my villa for as long as you want. Juan and I won't be back for weeks."

Shona made it all sound so easy, but it wasn't. Rachel might love Jed but she also loved her job and her life back home. There were her daughters to think of for one. The last two days she'd been battling with herself, trying to work out what to do.

"Make up your mind, Rachel. You are scheduled to return tomorrow, and I know Jed doesn't want you to go."

"I don't want to go either, but I have no choice."

At that point another voice joined the conversation. "Perhaps I can make it easier for you."

Rachel spun round — Jed had heard every word. "What d'you mean? How can you do that?"

"By telling you a story. Want to hear it?"

Rachel wanted more than anything to believe what he told her, for him to convince her that he'd had nothing to do with the traffickers. She watched him walk off, take a bottle of champagne from a waiter and beckon her to a table. He poured two glasses and took a sip. She was falling for it again, the old Jed charm. Still, it would do no harm to hear what he had to say. She sat opposite him and took a sip from the crystal flute.

"How much do you really know about the Ronan Blake case?" he began.

"As much as anyone does. Most of the gang is dead, Leonora is in witness protection and the big boss man is still on the loose," she said.

"You've got that wrong. Leonora Blake is dead."

"I don't believe you. She's hidden away with a new identity for her own safety, not that I agree with it."

"Me neither, but she is dead, and before you accuse me, I didn't kill her. She was found in a shallow grave in Staffordshire with a man called Baslow."

Rachel stared at him, not understanding. For a moment she thought all the champagne she'd drunk today had addled her brain. Had she heard him right? And if she had, how could Jed possibly know that? And where had he got the name Baslow from? She tried to process what he'd told her. Baslow dead? It had always been a possibility, but he had nothing to do with Jed or the Blake case. "Someone is feeding you information," she said at last, "that they're keeping from me."

Jed said nothing for a few moments and then he nodded. "I'm afraid you're right."

Rachel wasn't going to take this new information at face value. "Do you mind if I take a minute to confirm what you've just told me?" she asked.

"Be my guest." He smiled at her. "I'll sit here and let the cop in you do her job."

Rachel took her mobile from her bag, scooped up the long skirt of her gown and walked over to the balcony overlooking the sea. A word with Elwyn was needed. Urgently.

Without bothering with pleasantries, she asked, "Is Leonora Blake dead, found with Baslow in Staffordshire somewhere?"

There were a few seconds of silence. "Did Jude ring you?"

"Just answer me. Is it true?"

"Yes. Kenton told me but he ordered me not to tell anyone else. You're on holiday, so it didn't seem fair to bother you with it."

"It's okay. You don't have to make excuses. Thanks, Elwyn, I'll ring you later."

Rachel went back to Jed. She felt sick. Jed knew these things and she didn't. The truth was obvious, the only way Jed could know about the killings was if he was involved, if he was responsible for the deaths, or knew who was.

"I want the truth. How did you know? Is it because you ordered the killings yourself?" Her voice was cold.

"Rachel! What do you think I am?"

"Sometimes I think I don't know you at all. I'm utterly lost. You can't possibly know what happened to Leonora unless you had something to do with it. And as for Francis Baslow, I can't begin to work that one out!"

"I promise you, Rachel, I didn't have anything to do with it." He patted the seat beside him. "Come and sit down, and I'll explain it to you."

There was no way Rachel was going to listen to any more of his lies. "I'm sorry, Jed, I can't. I'll say my goodbyes to Shona and then I'm going to the villa and packing my stuff. The wedding is over, no need for me to stay. I'll get a flight home later tonight."

"You're making a big mistake not listening to me."

"I've heard enough, Jed. You haven't changed at all, have you? You're the same old Jed, with the same old problem. Do you know, I hope you are picked up soon and that you get the book thrown at you."

"That won't happen. And you should hear me out. You'll regret not listening. I can help you."

"I doubt that very much."

"Tell me, Rachel, during your investigations have you come across the name, 'GoldStar?'"

Rachel walked off, missing his final words. Jed had disappointed her yet again and she was too upset to listen to any more of his tales.

CHAPTER THIRTY-TWO

Elwyn didn't know what to make of the call from Rachel. He had no idea how she'd found out about Blake and Baslow, but he didn't have time to dwell on it now. He said nothing to the team, he needed their input on other matters.

"The bones found in the incinerator are not those of Sam Graham," he told them. "Whoever it is had their knee joint replaced at some time. I've checked with Graham's mother and she confirmed that he had never had such a procedure."

"So who is he?" Jonny asked.

Elwyn spread his arms. "God knows, son. We don't even know if the poor sod has anything to do with our case or not."

"Sam Graham hasn't been seen since he parked up some time ago. That strikes me as suspicious," said Amy.

"I think you're right and that takes us back to this being an inside job. Maybe Graham was the killer. The problem is, we have no idea where he's gone," Elwyn said.

"We can circulate a description and the press can run with it. We can ask his mother to get us a photo. It shouldn't be hard," said Amy.

"Good idea. Get it sorted. Go and see her, Amy, and while you're there get a DNA sample from her. We might get a familial match with the blood Jude's people found in Wignall's house."

"Will do. I'll take it straight to the lab and tell Jude it's urgent."

Elwyn got himself a coffee and sat at his desk. How had Rachel known about Blake and Baslow? Had Kenton rung her? The stand-in super wasn't in, or he'd have gone and asked him. For now, he had the more pressing murder case to concentrate on. He picked up the phone and rang the techies.

"Would you find out whose mobile it was that pinged the mast nearest to Knight's veterinary practice in Marple two nights ago and send me a list of names and numbers, please? It's urgent," he said.

"You're thinking Graham lured someone out there to take his place?" asked Jonny.

"If this is down to Graham, he planned it very well. He wants us to believe the burned body is his, so we run around like headless chickens and eventually stop looking," Elwyn said.

"I've been looking at the Woodsmoor account," said Jonny. "There was a fortune in it a couple of months ago, now it's empty. I'm trying to trace what happened to it, but one thing I do know, it didn't end up with Francis Baslow."

"Are you sure about that?" Elwyn asked.

"Yes. The money was transferred to a bank in the Channel Islands, and they've never heard of Baslow."

"He could have used a false name," Elwyn said.

"It wasn't him. The person who opened the account was a woman."

* * *

It was gone ten at night when Rachel arrived at Manchester airport. The flight from Malaga had been delayed, which meant it was too late to catch the team at work. Her head was buzzing. She still couldn't work out how Jed had known about the two deaths, unless he was involved. But if he was, why tell her? Was it some sort of warning?

It was raining and cold, vastly different from the sunny warmth of Spain. Head down, pulling her case behind her, Rachel headed for the taxi rank.

A man called out to her. "Rachel King?"

Rachel turned to look. Waiting at the pick-up point was a sleek black sports car. She'd no idea who he was so carried on walking.

"Ms King, I've been sent to pick you up."

Rachel stopped and looked at the car again. Who'd sent him, she wondered, the only person she'd told she was returning early was Alan. It had to be him. Given the appalling weather, he must have arranged it. *Very thoughtful.* "Did Alan send you?" she asked.

"Get in out of this rain," he urged.

Rachel pushed her case into the space behind the passenger seat and climbed in. "You didn't answer my question. Who are you?"

"That's not important, Rachel. I simply thought it was time we met."

"Why? I don't understand."

"I know what you do and I think we can be beneficial to each other. I was thinking a reciprocal arrangement. I help you and in return, you help me. I have one or two similar relationships with people in the police but I'm always looking for new people to work with."

He was older than her. Rachel put him at about sixty. It was dark and difficult to tell, but he looked like the third man in the photo Winnie had given Jonny. If he was, that made him a very dangerous individual indeed.

"What are you getting at exactly?"

He laughed. "I think you know, I'm talking about mutual aid, Rachel. I wouldn't expect you to help me for nothing, you'd be amply compensated."

"What's your name? You know me, but I can't place you."

"All in good time," he said.

He wasn't giving anything away. "Help you in what way? What do you want from me?"

"Nothing much to begin with." He gave her a reassuring smile. "A little information, a nod here and there, so that my people don't mess up. In return I'll help you in the same way. I could do wonders for those clear-up figures you people worry so much about."

"And you have these arrangements already? With colleagues of mine? Close colleagues?" she asked.

"Yes, and it works well. You'd be surprised what people will do for money, even those who should know better."

"It sounds like a proposition I might consider." Rachel was doing her best to sound calm, even interested. She had to find out more. "Who in particular has helped you in the past? Anyone I know?"

He shook his head, laughing. "Yes, but I'm not divulging any names, it would be breaching a confidence. Once we have you onside, it wouldn't do if the people you work with found out, would it?"

Had her onside! Rachel was quietly raging. This made today just about one of the worst ever. "Can I ask why you think I might be a likely candidate for this *offer* of yours?"

"Rachel, Rachel. You disappoint me. I was hoping you'd join us. It would make everything so much simpler."

They were on the airport link road heading towards the junction with the A6 that would take her home. She could make her own way from here. "Would you pull over please. I'm getting out."

"Sorry, I seem to have misread the situation. Please accept my apologies."

Standing at the side of the busy road, Rachel asked again, "Why me? You didn't say."

He looked up at her from the driver's seat, his eyes cold, his voice and expression hard. "Because you have a lot to lose, Rachel. Two lovely daughters for starters."

He pulled away fast, splashing Rachel with rainwater. She felt sick. She daren't ignore his words. She had to get home, make plans. The dual carriageway was busy. She trudged along the narrow path that led to the A6 roundabout, where hopefully she'd get a bus. That man had threatened her kids. If he was the one in charge of the trafficking ring, then he meant it. He could take her kids and spirit them away in a heartbeat, and they'd never be seen again. She couldn't take that risk. Despite the arguments and the ill-feeling, there was only one person she trusted to keep them safe.

CHAPTER THIRTY-THREE

Day Eight

Despite it being a Sunday, Rachel arrived at work early the next morning to find her team already hard at it.

"We weren't expecting you until much later today," Elwyn said. "Everything okay? You look a bit . . ."

She nodded at the others and beckoned Elwyn to her office. "I need a word."

Rachel dumped her briefcase on the floor and hung her jacket on the back of her chair. "I look like this because I've not slept a wink. My life's a bloody nightmare, Elwyn."

"What's happened?"

"Yesterday, you told me that Baslow and Blake were dead. How did you know?"

"Kenton told me."

"And we're investigating?" she asked.

"No. Look, I feel bad for not telling you but he said to keep it quiet for now. You were on holiday, and I didn't think it fair to bother you with it."

Rachel shook her head. "I'm not blaming you, Elwyn. Has Kenton said anything about the killings since? Like who is investigating, for example?"

"He's said nothing to me. They were found in Staffordshire. Mind you, Jude was asked for her input."

"Has there been any liaison with Stafford?" Rachel asked.

"Not that I'm aware of," he said.

"Doesn't that strike you as odd? Two murders related to the Blake case and nothing is being done about it. I want to know why that is. Is Kenton afraid we might find something? And what?"

"Hang on, Rachel. It was Salford's case originally. Why not have a word with Kenton before doing or saying anything rash."

"Because Kenton is sneaky. I've never trusted the man. I haven't since the day he walked in here."

"Trust issues aside, how did you know, Rachel? Did Jude ring you after all?"

"How I found out doesn't matter for now, but it wasn't from Kenton or Jude."

"Then I'm lost," Elwyn said.

"Have you had that photo blown up, the one Wignall was hiding, of the three men?"

"You've got a copy on your phone," he reminded, sounding puzzled.

"It's not high res enough."

"Okay, I'll get it for you."

While Elwyn was gone, Rachel flipped through the latest notes on the Woodsmoor case. Plenty happening, but progress was slow.

Elwyn returned minutes later and handed it to her. "This one isn't clear either," he said. "It's very blurred. Not up to Wignall's usual standard."

Rachel took it and studied the image for a few seconds. "I was stopped by a man at the airport last night. I was outside looking for a taxi and he offered me a lift."

"Not a good idea, accepting lifts off strange men," Elwyn said, and laughed. "Didn't your parents ever warn you?"

"He seemed friendly enough, knew my name. We meet so many people, I didn't think too much about it." She passed the image back. "It was him, Elwyn, the man with no name. I'm sure of it."

"And you got in a car with him? Someone we suspect of having dealings with Ronan Blake and Danulescu?" Elwyn sounded horrified.

"Stupid, I know, but I was curious."

"What did he want? I take it he didn't just happen to be there."

"He offered me a deal, wanted me to join a little gang of informants he has. He told me that he has similar arrangements with colleagues of mine."

Elwyn said nothing for a while. "Other officers? Maybe even people we work with?" His voice had dropped to a whisper. Rachel nodded. "Did you get any names?"

"No, he wouldn't tell me, but thinking about it overnight, I bet one of them is Kenton."

"That's a big leap. You can't go throwing accusations like that around, Rachel."

"The man made threats against my girls. He said I should join him because I had a lot to lose if I didn't." She paused for a moment, the realisation of what this meant hit her like a kick in the guts. "Truth is, Elwyn, I'm worried sick."

"You have to report it, Kenton first. He can help ensure your girls' safety."

"Like he did with Leonora Blake? No, Elwyn, I don't trust him. As I just said, for all I know he's on that man's payroll himself."

"So what do we do? We can't pretend this hasn't happened. There's no way you can deal with this alone."

"I don't intend to. Jed will take care of the girls. I rang him last night and he caught a flight here first thing this morning. Jed will take them somewhere safe until I've sorted this."

Elwyn was astonished. "You mean you trust McAteer but not Kenton, your senior officer?"

"Jed is Mia's father. Regardless of what goes on between us, he would never allow any harm to come to them. I do trust him, Elwyn. He won't let me down."

"I hope you're right, Rachel."

She nodded at the photo. "We have to find that man. He worked with Ronan Blake, and it was probably him who terrified Wignall — the car he was driving last night fitted the description. When I got out, I was shaken I admit, but I still had my wits about me." She smiled. "I got the registration number of the car."

"Give it to me, I'll run it through the system."

While Elwyn was away, Rachel sat down at her desk with the Woodsmoor file. Finding Sam Graham had proved to be tricky. If he wasn't the body in the incinerator, then who was it? And had Graham killed him and the others? She saw from the notes that Graham was now their prime suspect, but they'd no idea where he'd gone. His car was with Jude, hopefully she'd find something they could use. He had to be found soon if they were to put this case to bed.

Elwyn came back into her office. "The car is registered to a company called GoldStar."

"That name keeps cropping up. I first saw it written on the Blake file Kenton had."

"It's Kenton's case, Rachel. You have to tell him about this man and what happened to you last night. Whoever he is, he's made threats and you can't ignore them."

"I've not ignored them. Once Jed tells me they are all safe, I'll have a word with Kenton. But it's not that simple. My instincts tell me there's a lot wrong with the way Kenton operates. Supposing he's involved?"

"Tell him. He's your senior officer. He's in a far better position to arrange protection for your girls."

"We can't be sure of that. Let's see if we can find out more about the mystery man ourselves." She saw Elwyn's expression. He was unconvinced. "Give me an hour, a few more enquiries and then I'll speak to Kenton."

Elwyn nodded. "Wignall was keeping an eye on the GoldStar website, kept checking it although there's nothing on it. Jonny reckons it's just a landing page to show willing."

Rachel looked at the notes. "If that was the case, why would Wignall hide his laptop? It doesn't make sense."

"Apart from photos, Rachel, there was nothing else on it."

"It says here that it was hidden in the bedroom. Was there anything else?"

"Sentimental stuff, a couple of letters his mother wrote to him. Some family photos and cheap jewellery, which we presumed belonged to his mother too."

"Let's take a look."

They made their way to the evidence room, where the items taken from Wignall's house were quickly retrieved.

"This is the laptop, the other bag is here," Elwyn put it in front of her. "Jonny reckons he went through it."

"I don't doubt he did, but he presumed that the thing Wignall didn't want to be found was that." She nodded at the laptop. "But Wignall was clever. Let's see what else we've got here."

The letters yielded nothing — they were old ones from when Wignall had done time inside. The photos appeared to be family members — Rachel recognised one of his sister. But one was out of place, it wasn't of a person but a of a single piece of jewellery, a silver pendant. Rachel spread the jewellery out on the table. There were a couple of cheap rings, brooches, a silver chain and there it was, the pendant with a large green stone. It was unusual, old and not in keeping with the other cheap tat.

"See this?" She held it up and shook it. "Wignall photographed it for a reason. The stone is set in silver, and it's loose. Have you got a coin?"

"Let me." Elwyn took it from her and prised off the back. The green stone dropped out. Behind it there was a little memory card. "Well done! That was a brilliant call," Elwyn said. "Let's see what's on it."

* * *

Jonny put the phone down. He'd been speaking to the technicians about phone calls made in the area of Knights about the time of the murder. The results were simple — there had only been one. Connor Young's mobile had pinged the nearby mast, and the number he'd called was Kirsty's.

Jonny wanted a word. He needed to know what Connor had said to her, and why Kirsty had said nothing about it to them.

"I'm off to see Kirsty Mallory," he told Elwyn. "It's possible the body in the fire is Young. His mobile was used in that vicinity at the right time."

"In that case, you should check with Young's family whether he'd had a knee replacement. That'll confirm things," Elwyn said.

Hopefully, Kirsty would know. If he had, there'd be a scar and she'd have seen it.

"Want me to come with?" Amy asked. "I don't seem to be doing much here." She nodded to Rachel's office. "That pair are at it again, whispering and keeping stuff from the rest of us."

"I'm sure it's not like that, Amy," Jonny said.

"Oh, I'm sure it is, she doesn't trust me for starters."

"Rachel has a volatile personality, we've all felt the rough edge of her tongue. But mostly she's okay."

"You don't understand. I messed up just before she went away, I'm waiting for the flak to hit. I did something and she could have my job for it."

"She won't do that. Rachel's made plenty of mistakes herself. Want to talk about it?" he asked.

"No. It's not up for general discussion."

* * *

Kirsty Mallory looked no different than the last time Jonny had seen her. She wore the same dressing gown and the same suspicious frown.

"Tell us about the last time you spoke to Connor," Jonny said.

She shrugged. "Can't remember when that was."

"Don't play games, Kirsty. He was out Marple way, he rang you. He must have told you where he was going."

She looked surprised. "How d'you know that — him being in Marple?"

"Technology that's how. Come on, Kirsty, what did he tell you?"

She gave a resigned sigh. "He'd got a call earlier that day. It was some man. He wanted to buy dope off him, a lot. Connor said it was an opportunity, a deal worth thousands. The man said he'd pay him cash that same night."

"He arranged to meet this man?"

"Yep. The man said he would phone him with an address, and Connor left here in his car. Then I got that one call from him. He told me he was in Marple and fed up waiting about. He didn't reckon the man would turn up."

Jonny realised that Connor's car hadn't been found. It was possible that the killer, Graham, had driven it away from Knight's, leaving his own to be found by the police. If so, they should look for it.

"I don't know anything else," Kirsty continued. "I never saw or heard from Connor again. I presume he got the money and did one. Scared of you lot, he was."

"We don't think that's what happened, Kirsty," Jonny told her gently. "Did Connor have an old operation scar?"

"What's that got to do with anything?"

"Just answer the question," Amy said.

"Yeah, he did. On his knee. He had an accident on his motorbike and had to have a new knee joint put in."

"Do Connor's family live locally?" Amy asked.

That rattled her. "Why? What's happened? What d'you want that witch for? He's not seen her in years. I doubt she'd even recognise him now."

"We need her address. We believe Connor has been murdered," Amy said.

CHAPTER THIRTY-FOUR

Elwyn inserted the memory card into an adaptor then plugged it into his laptop. There were two files, one of them a 'Word' document a couple of pages long. It was a sort of testament from Wignall, stating that he'd been following a man called Daniel Rafferty, known as 'GoldStar,' a cover name for the people-trafficking ring. He admitted to driving for them and bringing young girls into the country illegally.

"Look. Wignall says that Rafferty is the head man," Rachel almost whispered, "not Jed."

"We need more if this is to stand up as evidence," Elwyn said. "Look at this paragraph. It is just what we need."

Wignall described CCTV evidence that he knew about. He stated that the girls had been unloaded from a container truck, like cattle, and imprisoned in a warehouse on an industrial estate in Ardwick. From there they were allocated to clubs, nail bars and other workplaces.

Elwyn was puzzled. "The CCTV was taken by a camera on that very warehouse. I can't believe that this Rafferty would be so careless."

"He'd still be wary of break-ins. Every other unit on the estate has CCTV cameras. Read on," Rachel prompted. "He writes that taking care of the footage was his responsibility.

Wignall was a photography buff, remember. Rafferty insisted that it was wiped daily but left the job to him. Wignall had the good sense to save this particular piece of footage, perhaps as insurance. Look, it's here, on the card."

The pair watched as the piece of film played out. Rachel was sickened. The girls were young, some no older than her own daughters. "See her?" she pointed to one of them. "That's one of the Eastern European girls we found working in Blake's club. Okay. You're right, we should hand this over to Kenton. I'll go and talk to him."

"I'll back this up first and then you can take it."

"What if he's involved, Elwyn? What do we do then? Because if he is, this evidence will not see the light of day."

"That's why I want to make a copy. We'll take it higher. But you have no proof that he is, and with respect, Rachel, your dislike of the man is down to his obsession with McAteer."

"Oh really? Nothing to do with walking in and stealing the Blake case, when we'd done most of the hard work? Remember that? No, I still don't trust him. I always get the feeling that he's keeping stuff back. He's far too secretive for my liking."

* * *

"I need to talk to you," Rachel began.

Mark Kenton gestured to a seat on the other side of his desk. "Nice break? Though I must say, Rachel, you look a little rough around the edges for someone fresh from the Spanish sunshine."

Cheeky sod! But she let it go. What she had to discuss was far too important.

"Daniel Rafferty."

The name hung in the air between them.

His smile was gone, replaced with a look of annoyance. "Who?"

"Don't play games, Mark, you know exactly who he is. Rafferty is the one behind the trafficking ring. I believe

178

you've known that all along. All your interest in McAteer was geared to throw me, and everyone else, off the scent."

He gave her a wry little smile. "It worked too, for a while. Rafferty has managed to elude the law for years. We'd finally worked out a way of catching him red-handed." He sighed, shook his head. "And then you blundered in."

"Me? What d'you mean? I was doing my job — unlike you!"

"I'm talking about the Blake case. Thanks to your interference, Rafferty had to close down operations, and quick. We lost all hope of catching the other members of the gang, or finding most of the girls. We had no evidence, so all we could do was wait and see if he started it up again. The problem was, did Rafferty know we were on to him?"

"And did he?"

"No, Rachel. We put a lot of work into making Rafferty believe we're after Jed McAteer."

"Was that down to Leonora Blake? Did she point the finger at Jed?"

He nodded. "She was trying to save her own skin, playing one side off against the other. Regardless of what we promised her, she would never feel safe. Rafferty has people everywhere and she wasn't willing to take the risk."

"You didn't keep her safe though, did you? How long after she went into witness protection did she end up dead, Mark?"

"There's no need for sarcasm, Rachel."

Rachel didn't know whether to believe what he'd told her or not. "So you set Jed up. You let an innocent man think he was wanted. He had to flee the country, for heaven's sake."

"Jed knew what he was doing. His actions helped enormously. It confirmed Rafferty's belief that we were on the wrong track. He relaxed his guard. He kept quiet for a week or two and then, as we thought, he resurrected his business. Now he's as active as ever."

"So arrest him."

"For that we need evidence, Rachel. None of his people will talk to us, and the trafficked girls aren't easy to find."

"I'm not having that. Haven't you heard of surveillance? Find out where he's working from, stop his lorries at the port." She handed him the memory card. "If you can't manage that, perhaps this will help."

"This is not your case and you should not get yourself involved." He looked at the thing in his hand. "What is this? I'm too tired to be solving riddles, Rachel."

"That, Mark, contains a statement from one Joseph Wignall, who drove a container lorry for Rafferty. There is also some CCTV footage you will certainly be interested in."

"Where did you get it?"

"Wignall is part of our Woodsmoor case. We found the memory card with his laptop, hidden in his house."

"Thank you. The investigating team will look at it."

"Team, Mark? Don't you mean you?"

"Drop it, Rachel. I don't want you mixed up in this. Get back to your own case. From what I've seen, it could certainly do with your input."

He wanted her out of the way. Well, that wasn't happening. "It's not that simple, Mark. I met Rafferty last night. He was waiting for me at the airport, and he offered me a lift home."

He glared at her. "I hope you didn't accept."

"Why not? Afraid of what he might have told me?"

"He's a dangerous man. You need to keep well away."

"Shame. Last night I hadn't heard your words of wisdom so I accepted his offer, but you're right, things did get tricky. During the trip home he offered me a job — as if I don't have enough on my plate." She laughed. "I demurred, obviously, but he intimated that if I didn't accept, he'd harm my girls."

Kenton's eyes widened. That had him rattled. "God, Rachel, what does it take? I've warned you off, you need to start listening. Rafferty is a big-time villain. He doesn't play around."

"He said there were colleagues of mine who worked for him. What d'you think of that, Mark? Can you throw any light on who he meant?"

His expression hardened again. Mark Kenton did not look happy. "You think I'm one of those colleagues? What do you take me for, Rachel?"

"Truth is, I don't know what to think." Rachel didn't expect him to admit anything at this point, she was just interested to see his reaction. But Kenton was a past master at not letting his true feelings show.

"First things first. Where are your daughters now?" he asked.

"Safe from harm."

"And you're sure of that? Rafferty isn't someone you fool easily. I can have them in a place of safety within the hour."

"Don't bother. I've made my own arrangements. I'll protect them myself. Mia was kidnapped once before, and I'm not taking any risks."

"You're making a big mistake. I can make sure that Rafferty doesn't find them, I promise you."

"Like he didn't find Leonora Blake," she said.

CHAPTER THIRTY-FIVE

Mia and Megan King had no idea what was going on. First thing that morning, Rachel told them to leave the house together as usual, and someone'd pick them up at the bottom of the road. She said she'd spoken to Jed the night before. He would meet them, and they were to go with him. They weren't to say anything to their dad — she would deal with Alan later.

Naturally they were puzzled, and the questions came thick and fast. Megan argued the toss but Rachel wasn't in the mood. She told her eldest in no uncertain terms that they had to do as they were told. It wasn't a game, their safety depended on it.

Mia was thrilled when she saw Jed's car waiting for them. "I don't know what's going on, but you'll get no argument from me."

Jed gave her a hug and ushered her and Megan into the rear seats. "I thought we'd take a trip to the coast. Sound okay?" he said.

"No can do," Megan told him. "This is all very exciting but I've got uni, and work to hand in. Why all the cloak and dagger stuff anyway? And why has no one said anything to Dad?"

"Your mother has organised this, and believe me, she would not drag us all away from our usual routines without good reason."

"Great. That means we're targets again." Megan nudged her sister. "Both of us this time."

But Mia didn't seem bothered. She got out her mobile. "Can I tell Ella where we're going?"

"I'm afraid not. In fact your phones must stay in my glove box. Give them to me."

The girls started to protest. "How am I supposed to find out what's going on at uni?" Megan demanded. "This is all very well but I've got exams coming up."

Jed handed each of the girls a new smartphone. "They're top of the range — you can do all the surfing you want on them. While we're gone, you'll use those and you only ring your mum and dad. That's it, no friends. Understand?"

They took the phones, though neither girl looked happy.

"It's Rachel's orders. Nothing to do with me. But she has a point."

"When will we be able to come back?" Megan asked.

"Your mum says a couple of days."

"We've got no stuff — no clothes, no make-up, and Mia doesn't have her insulin."

"Your mother thought of that. She's arranged for me to pick up a prescription at the local chemist. I'll get you both new stuff when we arrive at the hotel."

"You're him, aren't you?" Megan said. "That bloke from Mum's past, the one Mia reckons she's obsessed with."

Jed drove off, chuckling. "I'd like to think so, but you're wrong. We knew each other years ago. We're friends, but that's all."

* * *

Rachel checked her watch — eleven a.m. Jed and the girls should be well on their way by now. Kenton hadn't left his office. He had the memory card, he must have watched the CCTV — would he bring Rafferty in now?

"Harding's back later," Elwyn told her. "We've had an email."

"Do we know if he's any better?" Rachel asked.

"No, but he writes that he's returning to work forthwith. That'll put paid to Kenton's delusions of power."

"As long as Harding's not rushing things." She picked up the phone and rang Jude.

"Swanning off to Spain, eh? Hope you had a good time," Jude said.

"It was okay but too short. There's work to do here. The bodies, Leonora Blake and Baslow, did you get to examine them closely?"

"I helped with the PMs and brought back some samples which I intend to test," Jude said. "Why? What's on your mind?"

"They were killed on the orders of a man called Daniel Rafferty. I'm looking for a way of linking him to those bodies."

"Rafferty? That's a new one on me. Are we likely to find his details and DNA on the system?"

"I don't know, Jude, he keeps his head down and avoids getting mixed up with the law."

"If I knew what I was looking for . . ."

"Did Kenton give you anything to go on?" Rachel asked.

"No. He asked me to attend, help the pathologist and report back on how they were killed. Both were shot with a handgun — the same one. We have the bullets."

"And no attempt to hide their identities?"

"No. But they were buried in the middle of nowhere in the Staffordshire moorland. The chances of stumbling upon them were virtually nil."

"In that case, how did Kenton know they were there?" Rachel asked.

"He didn't discuss that with me, Rachel. I admit to being surprised, particularly when the male body turned out to be Francis Baslow."

Rachel made a mental note to ask him. "Can I see the reports?"

"Until I've done the tests there's not much to read. Kenton has them but I'll email them to you as well if you like."

"He isn't very cooperative — I'd prefer to get them from you."

"He hasn't commented as yet, or asked for further tests, so I can't say where the investigation is going." Jude said.

"Thanks, Jude. I'll get back to you."

Rachel had a bad feeling. How had Kenton known where those bodies were buried? She didn't want to believe that he was party to the murders, but what other explanation was there? And why did he want to keep the findings from her?

Jonny and Amy had returned from seeing Kirsty Mallory. "Bad news," Jonny said. "It looks like the body in the incinerator is Connor Young. He damaged his knee in a motorbike accident and had a replacement put in."

"Does he have family?" Rachel asked.

"A mother, but Kirsty has no idea where she is."

"Stella, try and find her. She should be told." Rachel looked at the time again. She was waiting for a call from Jed to confirm that they'd arrived. She wouldn't be able to relax until she knew her daughters were safely out of the way.

"Sam Graham. Any ideas? Amy, did you speak to his mother? Get that photo?"

"I called round, ma'am, but she wasn't in. A neighbour told me she'd gone away and won't be back until the weekend."

That wasn't any good. They had to give the press a photo today. "The Woodsmoor brochure — are there any photos of him in there?"

Jonny took it from his in-tray. He flipped through and passed it over, open at a page with a photo of two people. "That's Alison Longhurst. The man with her could be Graham."

"Did Larry Hardacre meet him?"

"Yes, ma'am, I think he did."

"Get round there with that brochure and check it out."

"It's not a good image. Graham's in the background, and there's a tree in the way," Jonny said.

"It's all we've got for now. If Mr Hardacre confirms that it's him, we'll see if the techies can help out," Rachel said.

Rachel's mobile rang in her pocket and she almost ran into her office.

It was Jed. "We're here and all's well. Don't worry, they'll be fine," he said. "They'll ring you later."

Elwyn had followed her in and immediately noticed her smart new phone. "That's new. What was wrong with your old one?"

"Nothing. This," she held it up, "is unregistered, a pay as you go. I've got a situation with Rafferty as you know. I thought it best to get the kids somewhere safe. I don't want our calls tracing."

"Who's with them?"

"Jed." Rachel saw the look. Elwyn didn't approve. "I trust him. He won't let any harm come to them. He wasn't behind the Blake case, Rafferty was."

"What about Kenton?"

"I'm not sure what his game is, Elwyn. I don't understand why he's not brought Rafferty in before now. It makes no sense. He knew about him, so why wait?"

CHAPTER THIRTY-SIX

Rachel was alone in her office, studying the PM report and what little there was in the ones from the Blake and Baslow murders.

Kenton barged in. "I need a word," he said. "You've got this all wrong. Whatever you may think, I've done nothing to help Rafferty. I want him brought to book, and I'd like nothing more than to be the copper who does it."

"So why protect him? I've just given you Wignall's statement and CCTV footage. Use it, Mark."

He sat down opposite her. "Wignall is dead. Nothing in that statement can be proved. It's his word against Rafferty's. As for the CCTV footage, it's not clear. The men in it are not easily identifiable and that warehouse they were using has gone. If you check, you'll find that it burned to the ground a month ago. Any forensic evidence we might have gathered from searching the place is destroyed. Rafferty has laid low, regrouped and found another site to operate from since then."

"You're doing it again, letting him get away with it. He had Leonora Blake and Baslow killed. Have you spoken to him about that?" she said.

"No. It would be pointless. I have no proof that he had anything to do with those killings."

"He was on that footage. He was in the photo Wignall put by for us. He was present when the bullets entered their skulls, I'll lay odds on it."

"You could be right, but we've still got no proof."

"Did CCTV pick up his vehicle on the Staffordshire roads at any time?" Rachel asked.

"He has a fleet of cars, hires most of them, so we've no way of knowing."

"It might be a slog, but isn't it worth a shot?" Rachel said. "He's still calling the haulage company he uses as a front 'GoldStar.' Anything there?"

"I doubt it. The company is no longer listed and we have no address."

"You have to do something. Sitting back and allowing that man to do as he wants is wrong. He is running a trafficking ring." She leaned forward. "Find out where he is operating from and catch him. And there's something else bugging me. How did you know where those bodies were buried? Jude reckons that without a tipoff they'd never have been found."

"Believe it or not, I had an anonymous call from a burner phone. The caller was male and no, I didn't recognise the voice, but it was heavily disguised."

That was altogether too convenient for Rachel's liking.

"I have another problem," Kenton said. My hands are tied. You'll have heard that Harding's back — well, he wants me gone. I'm clearing my desk and returning to Salford."

What a relief. "Knowing Harding like I do, when I tell him what we've got, *he* won't sit around on his backside watching Rafferty get away with it."

Kenton stood up and headed for the door. "Rachel, think carefully before you do anything rash."

Rachel threw down her pen and shut the file. She'd had enough of Kenton's attitude.

Her office phone rang, it was Jude.

"Have you seen the forensic reports on the two bodies?" Jude asked.

"I've skimmed through them, but I've been busy arguing the toss with Kenton."

"I've just had another look at the photographs and my notes. When he was shot, Francis Baslow was wearing a dark wool suit. We found fibres on it that didn't match anything he or Blake was wearing. They had to have come from the killer. I had another look at the sample we took of those fibres and I found traces of a third person's DNA on them. It definitely did not come from the victims."

Rachel smiled. "Does that mean we've got the killer's DNA?"

"Possibly, but you'll have to find that coat. You don't want to get to a court of law and have the killer maintain the coat was stolen. It was expensive, camel hair with fur — raccoon to be precise."

"Thanks, Jude, you're a star."

Rachel took the photo from the file. It had been taken in a Manchester street in the depths of winter. All three were wearing overcoats, but Rafferty's camel-coloured coat had a fur collar. With the evidence they already had, was this enough to get a search warrant?

Elwyn was at his desk when Rachel returned to the main office. "Have you seen Harding?" she asked. "Kenton is still using his office, so where has he gone?"

"Five minutes ago he was in the canteen," Elwyn told her.

Rachel scooted down the stairs.

* * *

Superintendent Stuart Harding sat on his own by the window, drinking coffee.

"Rachel! Nice to see you. How's the case going?" he said.

"We're getting there," she said. It was her standard reply. "How are you feeling? Any better for the treatment?"

"Indeed. The tablets are doing their job. I go back in a month for a small procedure and then we'll see."

He certainly looked better. She sat down beside him. "Do you recall the trafficking case, sir?"

"Yes, we're still looking for Jed McAteer, I believe."

"He's the wrong man. I think we were deliberately misled. The man leading the trafficking ring is someone called Daniel Rafferty."

Harding took his time considering this. "I'm aware that you were once, er, friendly with McAteer, Rachel. I hope this isn't some plan to get him off the hook."

Rachel was momentarily stunned. How could he think that of her? "I have proof, sir. And soon there will be DNA evidence to back it up."

Harding seemed nervous all at once, as if she'd touched a nerve. "You've discussed this with Kenton, I assume. It's his case, remember? I would hate our team to be accused of treading on toes."

"He is reluctant to act. I'm at a loss to understand his motive, and I'm worried that he is protecting Rafferty in some way."

"Very candid, Rachel, but an accusation like that should not be made lightly. Do you want me to take action? Do you have any proof of wrongdoing on Kenton's part?"

"I've shown him what we've got and all he says is that it's not enough. He won't even bring Rafferty in for questioning."

"As I said, it's his case. He must have his reasons, and of course, he works out of Salford. It's out of my hands, I'm afraid."

Rachel was losing heart. At every turn, she was met with obstruction. Why would her colleagues not act? Rafferty's words echoed in her head. He had said some of them were part of his organisation, but not Harding, surely? Time to lay it on the line. "Very soon, I'll have sufficient evidence to get a search warrant for Rafferty's premises, including his home. I want to bring him here for questioning."

"I repeat, Rachel, it's not your case." He was beginning to sound angry.

"With respect, sir, it is. A man called Francis Baslow was found in that grave too — he'd been shot — and he *is* part of our current case. Whether I get him for anything else or not, I hope to prove that Rafferty killed him."

"Tread carefully, Rachel, Kenton will not like it."

CHAPTER THIRTY-SEVEN

"Alan has rung twice in the last ten minutes. He needs to speak to you urgently," Elwyn said when she got back to the office.

Rachel retrieved her usual mobile from her desk drawer and rang him back. "There's no need to stress, as I told you this morning. The girls are fine. Is there another problem?"

"Too bloody right there is. You've been done over," Alan said.

Rachel's stomach churned. "When?"

"I was out for an hour or so this morning, so it must have been then. I went round to tidy up after the girls and that's when I saw the damage. The patio doors at the back have been forced open and your place is a mess."

Rachel knew what this was — Rafferty's revenge for refusing his offer last night. She'd been right to send the girls away. Megan would have been at home studying for her exams, and that didn't bear thinking about. "Have you rung the police?"

"Yes. Very helpful. They gave me a crime number for the insurance. They might send forensics round, but not today. I told them that the place can't be left in this state, but apparently that's up to me."

"Do you know if anything is missing?" she asked.

"Difficult to say, there's so much damage. Ornaments broken, doors ripped off cupboards and all the tellies have been smashed, even the ones upstairs in the girls' rooms."

"I might be able to get our own forensic people to take a look. Don't touch anything until I tell you."

Rachel felt as if someone had kicked her in the stomach. She imagined Rafferty's people trampling through her home, violating her space.

"Problem?" asked Elwyn.

"The house has been done over. Now d'you think I was rash to send the kids off with Jed?" She strode off to find Kenton. This had to stop.

She stormed into his office. "Rafferty was as good as his word! My house has been trashed. Just as well there was no one there."

"I'm sorry, Rachel. You should have kept out of it, the man is dangerous. What happened today is just a warning."

"Know that for a fact, do you? Well you can tell your pal from me that it won't work. The time has come for him to watch *his* back."

"You're wrong, Rachel, I'm not working with him. What would I gain?"

"That's simple. Money. No doubt he pays well."

"I promise you, Rachel, this isn't what you think. Speak to McAteer, he'll put you straight."

He was getting ready to leave, all his files packed into boxes. She left him to it. What did he mean, ask Jed? What did Jed know that he wasn't telling her? Back in her office, Rachel phoned Jude again.

"I need that DNA from those fibres urgently," she said. "My house has been broken into — a lot of damage done, according to Alan. My girls could have been there, Jude, what then?"

"Jason will go and have a look. If they've left any evidence, he'll find it. But your girls, Rachel. You've got them safe?"

"I got them out of the way. They're with Jed."

"Good guy now, is he?" Jude said.

"I'm beginning to think so, Jude. I may have misjudged him."

"Leave those DNA tests with me. As soon as I have something, I'll ring."

Kenton had said to ask Jed, so that's what she'd do. It was all very well talking to him over the phone but she needed to see him, watch his body language.

"I'm going out. I might not be back until late. Don't wait for me, Elwyn. I'll catch up in the morning."

"What if anyone asks?"

She smiled grimly. "You've no idea."

* * *

Jed had taken the girls to a hotel in Beaumaris on the Isle of Anglesey. With the traffic on her side, Rachel calculated that she'd make it in a couple of hours. She had also calculated that Rafferty's people might follow her, so she'd taken a pool car.

The drive gave her time to think. Despite trusting the safety of her daughters to Jed, she still believed there was something going on where he was concerned. He knew more than he'd been telling her. Well, today she'd force him to come clean. She'd had enough. She couldn't go on living like this. The Rafferty case had to be wrapped up quickly. She wouldn't settle until he was behind bars.

The hotel was large and expensive. Jed had got them a suite, a room for him with an adjoining room for the girls.

"It's proper posh," Mia enthused, "and we're having the best time."

Megan rolled her eyes. "Depends on your point of view. Personally, I'd rather pull my fingernails out. It's so boring my brain won't function anymore."

"Is there a problem?" Jed asked Rachel.

"Yes. I haven't come all this way because I fancied the ride. We need to talk."

"We'll go down to the bar. Don't dare leave this room," he warned the girls. "I'll take you both for a meal later."

They took the stairs. "Are they behaving?" Rachel asked.

"Sort of. Megan isn't happy. She doesn't like me much. She thinks I'm scuppering any chance of you and Alan reconciling."

"That ship sailed years ago, and anyway, he's got Belinda."

They sat at a table away from the other drinkers. Jed ordered a bottle of wine. "What's troubling you, Rachel?"

"Rafferty. He won't let up and I don't have enough to charge him with yet. You know something — the name of the police officer who's on his payroll for example? I have to know, Jed. He'll be arrested and provide evidence I can use against Rafferty."

"He might, but I wouldn't bank on it."

"Is it Kenton? He's dragging his heels and I don't understand why. The very least we should have done is interview Rafferty by now."

"It isn't Kenton," he said. "He's as straight as they come."

"So why doesn't he act?"

"He's baiting a trap. There is an informant in your station and Kenton knows who it is. When he tells you the evidence against Rafferty is flimsy, believe him. He's had dealings with the man and his legal team before."

Rachel was finding this difficult to believe. "If not Kenton, then who? A man like Rafferty would need someone with clout. And how do you know this anyway? How come you're privy to these underhand goings-on and I'm not?"

"For a while I had dealings with Ronan Blake." He held up a hand. "To do with property, nothing else. But I have a reputation, and he trusted me more than he probably should have. He told me things. I found out that he was involved in the trafficking and warned him off. It's a dangerous business and if you're caught, it's a long sentence. But he'd have none of it, said the big boss had a friend watching his back. A high-ranking policeman at your station, Rachel."

That meant Jed was right. "Kenton wasn't at our station until the case was well advanced. He worked out of Salford."

"You jumped to that conclusion all on your own, just because you don't like the man. He does have an edge to him, doesn't he?" Jed smiled.

"So why not put me right, Jed? For Christ's sake, you know how important this is to me, and now it's personal. You were blamed, everyone thought you were at the head of that ring. You had to flee or be arrested. What was that all about then?"

"Kenton wasn't sure who the police mole was, but he gave me the nod that I was top of the list of suspects and advised me to leave."

Rachel was gobsmacked. "Kenton did that?"

"He needed time and he wanted Rafferty to feel safe, to believe that his name was not associated with the trafficking. It worked too."

"So tell me, which of my esteemed colleagues is in Rafferty's pay? Don't clam up now, Jed. You know the truth and I want to hear it."

"Can't you work it out?"

"My head's spinning and I'm too tired to think straight," she said.

"Haven't you ever wondered why Harding didn't have your scalp over the Brough case and your involvement with me? He just stepped back and let it pass. There were no awkward questions about how we knew each other, or if you knew about my reputation."

"Harding?" Rachel exclaimed. "You can't be serious, Jed. The man's ill for a start. He can't be working for Rafferty."

"I promise you he is. At this very moment, Mark Kenton is trying to work out how to get Rafferty without alerting him and having evidence go missing."

"I don't believe it of Harding. You must've been misled," Rachel said.

"Then you're a fool. Kenton is a good detective. Don't you think that he'd have had Rafferty behind bars by now if it were at all possible? But each time he tries, there's a hiccup with witnesses or the evidence, and the case collapses before it ever gets as far as the CPS."

Rachel took her mobile from her pocket and rang Jude. "I won't be back until tomorrow morning, but if anyone asks what evidence there is in the Rafferty case, tell them it concerns Wignall's laptop. Don't mention the fibres or the blood."

"You must have psychic powers, Rachel," Jude said. "Superintendent Harding has been trying to contact me about that very topic. Fortunately, I wasn't here."

"Don't tell him the truth, Jude. Play everything down. It's important. I'll explain when I see you."

She turned to Jed. "It looks like you were right." Next, she rang the incident room and spoke to Jonny. "Get the hard drive from Wignall's laptop copied, but keep it to yourself, don't even let on to the boss. I've a feeling he'll be asking for that laptop very soon."

Rachel looked at Jed long and hard. She knew when he was lying, and now he was telling the truth. He'd worked with Kenton in an effort to bring down Rafferty and out the informant. "One last question for the time being. How did you know Leonora Blake was dead?"

"Kenton told me."

CHAPTER THIRTY-EIGHT

Day Nine

When Rachel came in the following morning, Elwyn told her that Harding had been looking for her.

"I had things to do," she said. "Want to know what evidence we'd gathered, did he?"

"He thinks we're going off at a tangent with Rafferty. He wants us to concentrate on the Woodsmoor case and leave the trafficking investigation to Kenton."

Rachel nodded. "Okay. I don't have a problem with that. Has Kenton left us?"

"Yesterday afternoon, and Harding has reclaimed his office."

"Sam Graham? Do we have a photo yet?" she asked.

"Only from the brochure, and despite the techie's best efforts, it's not great. I doubt it'll do for the press," Elwyn said.

"His mother?"

Amy looked up. "I went round to the house again, ma'am. A neighbour told me she's coming back today. She should get home about lunchtime, so I'll go round and wait for her."

Rachel nodded. "Connor Young drove to Marple that night, and we haven't found his car. Get a description circulated and check the CCTV on the roads around Knights. It wasn't left at the scene, so for now, we'll presume the killer took it."

Rachel wanted to speak to Jude, so she went into her office and rang her on the phone Jed had given her.

"Jude, it's me, Rachel. Have you got anything?"

"All we have to link Baslow and Blake is the fact that the bullets came from the same gun. To link Rafferty to those murders I need a sample of his DNA to match with that on the fibres we found. The coat is vital too, find that and we're on."

Rachel wanted Rafferty for Baslow's murder. She had every right too, as he was part of Woodsmoor. For that she needed that coat. First things first — the search warrant. Rachel decided to go to see Malcolm Connell in person. He was a magistrate they'd used before and was more sympathetic than most.

"I'll be about an hour," she told the team. "Rafferty lives in Didsbury. Find out his exact address and text me. I'll get the warrant and meet you there. I want him bringing in. If Harding asks, don't tell him anything. Be as vague as you dare."

* * *

Malcolm Connell had helped Rachel in the past when she'd needed things to move quickly. Elwyn had sent her the address and she had the warrant in her hands within the hour. Back in her car, she checked her mobile again. There was nothing from Elwyn to say that he was in position. What was the holdup? She rang him.

"We've had Harding on the prowl. I'm sorry, Rachel, but I had to tell him where you'd gone. He is the super, after all."

"Damn that man! Okay, don't stress about it, Elwyn, just meet me at Rafferty's place before he does a runner."

She'd no sooner finished talking to Elwyn than her mobile rang. It was Harding.

"You have had a warrant issued to search Daniel Rafferty's property, I hear. Why, Rachel? What do you think the man has done?"

"He murdered Francis Baslow, sir," she said simply. "Baslow was one of the Woodsmoor three. I have enough evidence to charge him, so there shouldn't be a problem."

Harding fell silent. "Mistake," he said at last. "He is a dangerous man. You are taking a great risk crossing him like this."

"No one is above the law, sir, not even Rafferty, for all his bully-boy tactics."

"Have you told Kenton?"

"It has nothing to do with him. The arrest concerns my case. If he wants him, he can find his own evidence." Rachel ended the call. The traffic would be against her, and she needed to get to Didsbury before Rafferty had a chance to scarper.

* * *

Rachel found the Rafferty home in a private development of executive properties. The car he'd picked her up in was parked on the drive.

With Elwyn at her side and three uniforms for backup, Rachel approached the front door. The search team were waiting at the front gates for her signal.

An attractive and expensively dressed woman answered the door. She looked about fifty, and Rachel assumed she was Rafferty's wife. The expression on her face as Rachel flashed her badge suggested she'd trodden this path many times before, and didn't expect this journey to end any differently from the others.

She turned and called out, "Daniel! You have visitors."

Rafferty emerged, adjusting his tie. He smiled and nodded at Rachel. "I do hope this won't take long. My wife and I are about to see some friends."

"I'm afraid you'll have to cancel, Mr Rafferty. You're coming with us. And while you're away, my colleagues over there will search your house." Rachel showed him the warrant, made the arrest and read him his rights.

Rafferty was angry but doing his best to keep his temper under control. "Get Jonathan on the phone, Muriel, and tell him it's urgent." He turned to Rachel. "East Manchester in Ardwick, isn't it? Jonathan Murray is my solicitor. He'll soon put a stop to this rubbish."

CHAPTER THIRTY-NINE

When Rachel got back, Jonny was waiting for her. "DCI Kenton knows about the arrest," he said. "He didn't sound happy either. He's coming over."

Just what she needed! Well, he'd have to wait his turn. Rafferty was hers and until she'd finished with him, Kenton's questions would have to wait.

"The Rafferty property is being searched," she told the team.

"What are they looking for, ma'am?" asked Jonny. "I still don't understand what we've got on the man."

"Jude is with them, and she knows exactly what we want. I've had to keep the details quiet in case the evidence walked, which it has done in the past. Until I have confirmation off Jude, I'm still not saying. But it will be more than enough to satisfy the CPS. The best legal team in the country won't get Rafferty out of this one."

"Don't count on it. He's slipped through our net before." It was Kenton.

"Not this time, Mark, trust me. That man is going down."

He gestured to her office. "Can I have a word?"

Rachel shut the door and faced him. "What now?"

"Rafferty's solicitor has turned up. I don't know if you've had dealings with Murray in the past, but he's good. Very good."

"Get his kneecaps done if he doesn't win the day?"

"No, but he's impatient. You've had Rafferty in custody for an hour now, and he's still waiting. What's the holdup?"

Rachel felt nervous suddenly. What if Jude and her team didn't find the coat? What if it was at the cleaners or had been left somewhere else? "Jude Glover has her instructions. I'm waiting for a text or call from her, then I'll move."

"You're looking for something specific, aren't you, Rachel? Tell me. Perhaps I can help."

"I've told no one, only Jude, and I don't intend to until the evidence is safely in our hands."

Rachel was well aware that there would be a further delay once the coat was found. Jude would have to do her tests. Until they had those results, they wouldn't be able to charge Rafferty.

"Look, I'd appreciate you getting off my back, Mark. The next few hours are crucial and I don't need you bending my ear."

"Okay, but the clock is ticking, and Murray won't let you keep him one minute longer than you are allowed."

Rachel had worked that one out for herself. What was keeping Jude? She returned to the main office. "Elwyn, you and me will make a start. I'm still waiting for a call from Jude." She handed her mobile to Jonny. "The minute she rings, you come and get me."

* * *

Daniel Rafferty seemed to find the whole thing enormously amusing.

"Quite a pantomime this, isn't it? What do you think I've done, Rachel?" He leaned forward slightly. "You don't mind if I call you Rachel, do you? Only, after I picked you up at the airport, rescuing you from the rain, I thought we were friends. You obviously got home okay. I was quite concerned. I shouldn't have let you go off into the night like that."

Ignoring all this, Rachel asked, "Tell me how you first met Francis Baslow."

"I've no idea who you're talking about. Sorry, you must have me confused with someone else."

"He was found in a popular dumping ground of yours in Staffordshire. He'd been there about three months."

"Not me, love. No way. You see, Rachel, I don't kill people."

Murray intervened. "DCI King, do you have evidence to back up this accusation? It's pretty serious. If you do have anything, produce it, or let my client go."

"Baslow was buried with Leonora Blake. You do know her, she and her husband ran one of your dives."

Rafferty smiled. "Yes, I do recall Leo. Great woman. Muriel my wife was very fond of her. Don't tell me she has met with an unfortunate end too? Tut-tut. What is the world coming to?"

Without the coat, they were doomed. They had no other evidence and this pair would run rings around them. Rachel called a temporary halt to proceedings and went back to the office.

"Get Jude on the phone," she barked at Jonny. Arms folded, Mark Kenton was sat at Amy's desk. "The evidence we got from Wignall, his statement and the CCTV . . ."

"I wouldn't, Rachel," Kenton said. "Murray will tear it to shreds. I've looked at that footage. It's grainy, the figures are indistinct. You can't prove that it's Rafferty on that film."

Jonny held the phone out to her. "Dr Glover, ma'am."

"Jude. Have you found it?"

"We've searched the house from top to bottom. It's not here, Rachel. I'm sorry, but there's nothing more we can do."

Rachel felt like screaming. The match between the fibres on that coat and those on Baslow's body was crucial to making the murder stick. "Are you sure there's nowhere else you can look? What about his car?"

"It's on the drive, I'll get the keys and ring you right back."

Rachel put the phone down. This was hell.

"Evidence gone walkabout?" Kenton asked.

Rachel glared at him. "That's not possible. I hadn't told a soul what I was looking for."

Her mobile rang again. "That was inspired, Rachel," Jude said. "It was in the boot. I've got it here. It's exactly what I thought, an expensive camel-hair number with a raccoon-fur collar. But what's even more interesting are the faint blood marks on the front, all smeary. It looks like someone has had a go at cleaning them off."

"Get it tested, Jude. Speak to you later."

CHAPTER FORTY

"What now?" Kenton asked.

"We wait. Jude's doing more tests and then, hopefully, I can charge Rafferty with Baslow's murder."

"And Leonora Blake?"

"That depends on what Jude finds."

"You'll run out of time," Kenton said. "Murray will count every second of the twenty-four hours you're allowed to keep Rafferty in custody. Apply for an extension and he'll fight you all the way."

"The evidence we have is robust. Believe me, Mark, we will get that extension, and we will definitely need it so Jude can complete the tests."

Now came the worst part — the waiting. Rachel retreated into her office to think. What she needed was something else to throw at Rafferty in the meantime.

Amy knocked on her door. "Graham's mother still isn't home. I've been virtually camped on her doorstep all morning, but no luck. A neighbour even asked me what I was up to!"

Rachel's head was too full of Rafferty to think coherently about the Woodsmoor case. "We'll have to leave it for now. Go with the photo we've got. See if you can get it in the evening edition and don't forget our online friends."

Kenton tapped on her door. "Murray is kicking up a fuss, insisting we've got nothing and accusing us of harassment. Do you want me to have a go? Against my better judgement, I could try some of the evidence you collected from Wignall's house — the statement, the CCTV footage. See what his reaction is. It might buy us some time, frighten him a little while we wait for your results."

"I don't think that's a good idea. He'll wriggle out of it. You said yourself, the footage isn't good enough and Wignall is dead. They'll dismiss his statement as the ramblings of a man too ill to think clearly — which he probably was," she added.

"Okay, we wait for the forensic evidence and get him on Baslow's murder."

Rachel nodded. "Once he realises he can't wriggle out of that one, you can move in on the trafficking case. If your officers have any statements from the girls we rescued, now is the time to dust them off."

"Want to join me?" he asked.

"No, I need to gather my thoughts for later."

* * *

Jonny Farrell had been pursuing a line of enquiry of his own. Jason Fox had rung the incident room with some interesting information about some receipts found in the boot of Graham's car. There was no doubt that the vehicle belonged to Sam Graham — his fingerprints were all over it, plus those of one other person, an unknown.

The receipts were for shopping done at a large supermarket in Ancoats. Several were for items paid for in cash but some had been paid with a debit card, and now he knew who that card belonged to.

He knocked on Rachel's door. Glancing through the window, he could see that she had her head down, intent on paperwork.

"Sorry to interrupt, ma'am," he began, "but I've got something."

"About the Baslow murder?"

"No, Woodsmoor." He put the receipts on her desk. "These were found in the boot of Graham's car. That one," he pointed, "was paid for by debit card."

"So? What are you getting at?"

"Not Graham's card, ma'am. It belongs to Beatrice Reilly."

That got Rachel's full attention. "They knew each other? Is that likely?"

"Alison Longhurst was Reilly's sister, and she and Graham did work together, but I still find it odd. Also, there's the bank account in the Channel Islands where the Woodsmoor money is languishing. That was opened by a woman."

"You think Reilly and Graham are in this together?"

Jonny nodded. "It's worth looking into, at least."

"Okay. Take Amy and a couple of uniforms and go round to Beatrice Reilly's place. See if she can give you an explanation." Rachel leaned forward to take a closer look at the receipts. "More than one was paid by debit card, and look at the dates — regularly, every week. I think you could be right, Jonny. When I went with Elwyn to inform her about Alison's murder, she had a man with her by the name of Len Partington." She was checking her notes. "Good work, Jonny. Keep me informed of what you find out." Jonny made to leave the office. "How's your dad doing, by the way?"

"He's home now and as cantankerous as ever. Last week he was at death's door, this week he's laying down the law as if nothing had happened."

* * *

"You're doing it again, wheedling your way into her good books," Amy said. "You make me sick, you do."

"I don't understand you, Amy. What do you want from the job?" Jonny retorted. "I for one want a career and I won't get that unless I make my mark. Rachel is okay. She clawed her way up the ranks and she knows the score. She recognises a trier when she sees one, so give it a go, show a bit more gumption and you might get a surprise."

"She's no fan of mine, believe me. Where are we going anyway, and why the backup?" She glanced over her shoulder at the police car following them.

"I did a bit of research and discovered something. We're following it up, that's all."

"If this was school, you'd be the teacher's pet! Come on then, what have you got?"

"If I'm right, I know where Graham is holed up."

"Jesus! I've spent most of this week trying to pin down his mother, in the hope of getting a handle on him. I hate you sometimes, Jonny Farrell."

CHAPTER FORTY-ONE

"Ready for the supermarket run, Len?" Beatrice Reilly asked. "Thought I'd do a big shop, get it done for the week. We can have a spot of tea while we're there, save cooking."

"I've got a lot on, love," he said. "A job's come up and I should go and see when the interviews are."

"Great news, Len." She kissed his cheek. "Hope you get it. You deserve a break."

All lies, if course. It'd been fun at first but now he was tired of all the pretence. Len Partington had served his purpose but there was no need for him anymore. It was time to get out. He hadn't brought much of his own stuff with him when he'd moved in, so moving out wouldn't be a big deal. It was just a case of keeping Beattie sweet until his plans were in place. "If I get it, we'll go out for tea somewhere posh, never mind the supermarket. Keep your fingers crossed. By the way, have you heard any more from the police about your sister?"

"No, and I'm getting annoyed. How long does it take, Len? Alison, Baslow and now Sam Graham. Surely they must know what's going on by now?"

"Perhaps they do. They don't tell the public everything."

"They're no closer to finding who killed them," she said. "I rang the station a couple of days ago, spoke to one of the detectives about interviewing the boys, and he gave me an update. Does my head in. I could find out the truth quicker myself."

"And the boys? Are the police going to interview them?" He knew it wouldn't make any difference if they did, neither of them had seen a thing.

"Possibly, but it'll only be Andrew. After all, he's the one who found his mum."

It was Partington who heard the knock on the front door. He spotted the police car through the window and hoped it was simply a courtesy call to keep Beattie in the loop. Nonetheless, he daren't take that risk. Time to make a quick exit. He snatched up his coat. "Visitors, love! See you later."

He left by the back door, through the garden and out the gate that led into the playing fields. He was busy fastening his coat against the chilly wind when he was grabbed from behind by a uniformed PC.

"Mr Graham?"

"It's Partington, mate. You've got the wrong bloke."

"I don't think so," Jonny said, hurrying up to join them. "You're coming down to the station with us."

"Jonny!" Amy called. "Connor Young's car is in the garage."

The supposed Partington's face contorted with rage. "How did you find out? This wasn't supposed to happen. I don't understand how you found me."

"Carelessness on your part," Jonny said. "A simple strip of paper left in your car."

Graham — for that's who he really was — shook his head. This wasn't right. The copper had to be bluffing, trying to get him to trip himself up. "I don't believe you. I don't make mistakes. I planned this to perfection."

"Not really. For starters, you left your prints and DNA all over Wignall's house."

"The notices on the street said they were beginning demolition that very week."

"It didn't happen," Jonny said.

He should have checked. It wouldn't have taken long to drive past, but he hadn't. "A strip of paper, you said?" Graham asked.

"A supermarket receipt, paid by debit card in the name of Beatrice Reilly."

Graham stared at him. "It was her that left it there, not me. Stupid bitch!"

* * *

Sam Graham was being processed prior to interview. "Well done, both of you," Rachel said. "Particularly Jonny, who found the vital piece of evidence."

"One down, one to go," Elwyn said, handing her a mug of coffee. "We'll interview Graham, get the details, the whys and hows, and then we can put the Woodsmoor case to bed."

"I want the Rafferty case to go exactly the same way, smooth and pain free at the end. It's doing my head in. I can't take any more of Rafferty's crap."

She checked the time. "We'll speak to Graham but we'll have to leave Rafferty until tomorrow. Jude's results should be in by then. We'll need that extension, Elwyn."

"Do you need a word with Harding?"

Rachel realised that amid all the pressure of bringing in and dealing with Rafferty, she hadn't told Elwyn about the super.

"Harding is on the take." Blunt, but why should she wrap it up? "He's on Rafferty's payroll."

She saw the look of utter disbelief on the sergeant's face. She could almost see the cogs turning — he must have thought she'd lost her mind.

"Harding is as straight as they come."

"No, Elwyn, he's not. That's why I've kept the evidence we were searching for to myself. I didn't want Harding to find out."

"Who told you this fairy tale?"

"Jed, but Kenton backed it up."

"And you believe them? You've been working with Harding for a long time. Surely, if he was selling us out, you would have noticed before now?"

"I have thought about it, Elwyn. The only reason I came up with is his illness and needing money for the treatment in the States."

"If you're wrong, there'll be hell to pay."

She changed the subject. "Will you interview Graham with Jonny?"

"Don't you want in?" he asked.

"I want to speak to Jude, and I'd be no good anyway, my head's too full of Rafferty."

"That was a waste of everyone's time," Kenton said returning to the office. "All I got out of Rafferty was 'no comment,' courtesy of his solicitor of course."

It was getting late, and Rachel was keen to go home. Alan wasn't happy about the arrangements regarding the girls, and would take some convincing that she'd done the right thing. "We'll lock him up until morning. I hope to God Jude gives us what we need then."

"Murray is complaining, wants to know what we have on his client and why we haven't produced it."

"Sod him! I'll have Rafferty taken to the cells and boot Murray out if I have to."

Rachel left Kenton in the main office. The day had been a mix of highs and lows, but right now she felt sick. She sat in the observation room watching, as Elwyn began the interview with Graham, who was being just as unhelpful as Rafferty.

* * *

"You've got it wrong! I haven't killed anyone," Graham yelled.

"In that case how come your DNA and prints are in Joseph Wignall's house?" Jonny asked.

"It's obvious. I've been framed. Someone has done this to me, probably one of those customers we swindled."

"Have you got anyone in mind?" asked Elwyn.

Graham took a slug of water and said nothing.

"Tell us what happened, Sam. Help us to understand," Jonny urged.

"You wouldn't understand. No one can. Something awful happened and I can't get over it."

Neither detective had any idea what he was talking about.

"She was all I had, all I needed. Mum said I was obsessed, but that wasn't it. I loved her." Graham started to cry. He took a tissue from the box Jonny offered and blew his nose.

Rachel realised that he was talking about the loss of his fiancée, Nina.

"What are you trying to tell us, Sam?" Jonny asked.

"We were getting married. There was no one like her, she was so special. I didn't want her involved in the Woodsmoor scam, in fact we argued about it. It was the only row we ever had."

"What exactly did you argue about?" Elwyn asked him.

"Nina inherited money from her parents. She wanted to do something for us both, and surprise me. She wanted us to leave the city and start again somewhere nice. I tried to tell her truth but I couldn't admit that we were ripping people off, that there was no 'perfect place' called 'Woodsmoor', and there never would be." He lowered his gaze. "She didn't listen. Nina went ahead behind my back, bought a property. Alison handled the sale and kept it quiet. I hated her for that. I rang Baslow, begged him to give Nina her money back, but he refused."

"Didn't that make you think about the other people you'd cheated? What you were doing was against the law. You were selling unsuspecting people property that didn't exist, that was never going to be built. Didn't you consider them?" Elwyn said.

"We sold the plots in good faith. Baslow said it was fine. Alison and I didn't realise what was really going on until it was too late. I wanted to get out, but we were making a lot of money."

"What happened to Nina?" Jonny asked.

"They killed her."

"How?"

"Not with their own hands, but they might as well have done. Nina couldn't bear the idea that she'd lost all her money and we could never have the future she wanted for us."

Elwyn knew. He'd been at Graham's house when his mother had told them about the fiancée who'd killed herself.

"What happened, Sam?" Jonny asked.

"Nina killed herself. She couldn't handle losing the money. I think she even blamed me for some of it. I found her dead in her bath, drowned. I swore then that I'd get even, make Alison and Baslow pay for what they had done to Nina and the others. She was a simple soul, my Nina. All she wanted from life was to marry me and have a place of our own. Baslow and Alison stopped that happening."

"You went from salesman to killer in a very short space of time." Elwyn said.

"I was raging, you've no idea how I felt. No one can understand. Baslow and Alison, they took from me the only thing I ever wanted, my Nina."

That explained the confetti and the removal of both victims' ring fingers.

"What happened to the money, Sam?" Elwyn asked.

"I took it. Transferred it from Baslow's account to one of those Channel Islands' ones. I got Beattie to set it up for me. She'd no idea what it was all about. Do anything for me, that woman would."

"And Baslow just gave you his bank details, did he? Seems a bit far-fetched."

"He was desperate. There were men after him. He said they'd mistaken him for someone else and were going to kill him. He'd taken another man's identity when he'd left hospital, for a while he even lived in his shed of a house. He rang me one night, saying he needed to disappear. I agreed to help." He gave a short laugh. "I was leading him on. There was no way I was going to help that man, not after what he did."

"What men? Who did he think were after him?" Elwyn asked.

"I didn't ask. He texted me the address of where he was holed up. I said I'd get him out but I wanted the money in the Woodsmoor account. He didn't hesitate, sent the account details straight back. He must have been truly terrified."

Jonny realised that he must mean Wignall's house. The men pursuing Baslow would have been Rafferty's people, because Baslow had gone there after leaving hospital, they'd mistaken him for Wignall. "This house, an old rundown property in Longsight?"

Graham nodded.

"You stayed there for a while?"

"I went to see if Baslow was finally gone. If he'd been taken. The place was in a state. But I'm not fussy, it was a good base while I carried out what I'd planned. I invented Len Partington and took up with Beattie to keep tabs on you lot."

"So you killed Connor Young," Jonny said.

"He got in the way, always hanging around. But I made good use of him in the end."

"We saw," Jonny told him.

"You killed Alison Longhurst, Connor Young and a man called Joseph Wignall," Elwyn said. "Of the three of them, only Alison had had anything to do with Woodsmoor."

"I killed Baslow too. He must have avoided the men chasing him, because in the end I tracked him down to that nursing home."

"No, you didn't. The man you killed lived in that house in Longsight you squatted in. It was him the men who threatened Baslow were after. If you'd met Baslow, you'd have realised your mistake."

"Baslow made that choice. He wanted to remain in the background. Neither me nor Alison ever met him." Graham shrugged. "I'd no idea he wasn't Baslow. Poor sod is better off dead anyway. That home was the pits."

CHAPTER FORTY-TWO

Day Ten

"Graham has been charged." Rachel beamed at the team. "Well done everyone. He led us a merry dance but it came good in the end."

"Rafferty next," Elwyn said. "Will that be today?"

"I hope so. Right now, I'm waiting for Jude. Until then he stays locked up."

"DCI Kenton is coming over, ma'am," Amy said. "He rang earlier."

Rachel knew what that was about, but she'd already decided that she would conduct the interviews together with Kenton. Kenton was hoping Rafferty would say something about Leonora that might lead him to the evidence he needed.

"Murray is here," Stella said. "I've put him in the soft interview room. He's not very pleasant, is he? No manners."

Rachel retreated to her office, desperate for Jude's call. The morning was going to drag.

"Everything okay at home?" Elwyn asked, coming in to join her.

"Alan wants the kids back. He doesn't understand why he can't protect them, why I've given the task to a man he doesn't even know."

"Alan's got a point," Elwyn said.

"Jed is the best person for the job, Elwyn, and that's the end of it."

"Are you and him back on then?"

Rachel pulled a face. "We might be. I haven't decided what I want. We had a lovely time in Spain, and it made me realise a lot of things. But it's a big decision and I'm not making it yet."

Rachel was about to say more when her mobile rang. It was Jude.

"I have your results. It's even better than we thought. It is Baslow's blood on that coat, tiny amounts, hardly noticeable to the naked eye. Plus there is no denying the coat belongs to Rafferty, he was tested on arrest and his DNA is all over it. Will that do you, Rachel?" she asked proudly.

"Jude, you are wonderful! I owe you big style."

"Yes, you do, old friend. I've worked all night on this. The report should be in your inbox by now."

* * *

When Rachel went out into the office, Kenton had arrived. "We're on!" she said, waving a printout at him. "Let's get this done." Rachel put the report back in the file, and in silence she and Kenton made their way along the corridor. Get this right and she would have brought down one of Manchester's most notorious criminals.

"Mr Rafferty." She smiled. "I trust you had a good night. Treating you well, are we?"

"Cut the crap, Rachel. I want out of here. Refuse and you won't like the repercussions."

"You're threatening a police officer. You know it doesn't work like that." Rachel put her file on the table and took out a photograph, the one of three men outside the Midland Hotel. "Tell me about this picture."

"Not this rubbish again. I had a bellyful with him yesterday. That's not me and I've no idea what's going on."

"It is you. That's your coat." Rachel tapped the picture. "And I know that for a fact, because we found it in your car when we did the search. Nice it is too, very distinctive — genuine camel hair with a raccoon-fur collar."

"Random photos, my coat. What have they to do with anything?" Rafferty said.

"I agree. Kindly explain yourself, DCI King," Murray said. "My client and I admit to being confused."

"Roughly three months ago, you killed a man by the name of Francis Baslow. You took him to a desolate spot in the Staffordshire moorlands and shot him."

Rachel waited.

Rafferty said nothing for several seconds. Then, "Not me. You're deluded."

"In that case, kindly explain how Baslow's blood got on your coat," Rachel said. "True, only minute amounts, but enough to send you down."

Murray's eyes widened. He cleared his throat. "I'd like a word with my client in private."

"All in good time," Rachel said. "Your people made a mistake. They took Baslow when they should have taken a man called Joseph Wignall. I'm surprised you didn't notice, Mr Rafferty. That's Wignall in the photo with you, so you had met him." She tapped it again.

"I have dozens of employees. I can't be expected to know them all."

"Not even when you're having them executed?"

Murray leaned towards Rafferty, most likely advising him not to say anything else.

"This evidence. It's watertight?" he asked.

"Absolutely."

"May we have a word with Superintendent Harding?"

Kenton said, "I'm afraid Superintendent Harding has been relieved of his duties, gentlemen. He is no longer a serving officer and so can be of no help to you."

This hit Rafferty hard. They saw his face redden. He looked as if he was about to explode.

"The whole thing should have been stopped before it got to this! Harding has let me down." He glared at Rachel. "You go rooting around my house, taking my things. How do I know I haven't been fitted up?"

"You were careless. Admit it. You even tried to clean the coat. There is evidence that it's been sponged. Fond of it, are you? Not able to part with it? You should have dumped the coat when you saw that blood. Or perhaps you thought yourself so above the law that it would never come to this."

"You might think this is a win for you," Rafferty levelled at her. "If the prosecution is up to it, I might even go down, but consider this, DCI King. Behind bars or not, I have a very long reach. I warned you once, but make no mistake, do this to me and your days are numbered!"

Murray coughed loudly in an effort to drown out Rafferty's words. "My client is overwrought. I'll have a word."

"You will be charged with the murder of Francis Baslow," Rachel said. "And now my colleague here wants to interview you about a different matter. We will talk again. If you want things to go well for you, I'd encourage you to give DCI Kenton all the help you can."

With that, Rachel got up and left the room, to be replaced by a DS from Kenton's team at Salford.

EPILOGUE

Twelve Weeks Later

Rachel was looking smart in a two-piece suit and with her hair freshly done. "Court," she told her colleagues. "It'll be a pleasure to watch Rafferty get his just deserts."

"Kenton have any luck with the Leonora Blake murder?" Elwyn asked.

"Rafferty has been charged on that score too. Those photos of Wignall's finally came into their own. He snapped every place they picked up the girls. Europol has helped Salford find some of them and those who met Rafferty will give evidence against him. Kenton intends to use the fact that Leonora was in the same grave and shot with the same gun. On the balance of probability, the jury might come to the correct conclusion."

Rachel went into her office to check her hair. She smoothed out the straight skirt, which was tight around her waist. Perhaps she should have worn something else.

"Don't fuss. You look great."

"You're a flatterer, Elwyn Pryce, but I know the truth. I'm a bag of nerves. I feel quite sick."

"You'd never know. You're positively glowing."

"Got our man, didn't we? Does wonders for the confidence," she said.

"The post of detective-super is up for grabs," Elwyn said. "Fancy going for it? As things are at the moment, you have to be up there with a chance."

Rachel gave him an enigmatic little smile. "It's not for me, Elwyn. Not yet awhile anyway."

"Why on earth not? Go for it. I would in your shoes."

Rachel considered this for a moment. Elwyn had a point. Ordinarily she wouldn't hesitate. She was ambitious and keen to get on.

"Is it McAteer? You're keeping it pretty quiet, but I know you're back with him. D'you think that might stand in your way?"

"No, I don't, Elwyn. Jed is seen as okay these days, and he's promised that's how it'll stay."

"Okay, I give up. What's stopping you going for the super's job?"

"I wouldn't have the time, and my mind will be on other things. More important things."

This was really not like her. "I don't get it," Elwyn said.

Rachel grabbed her briefcase and glanced in the mirror one more time. She'd have to do. Elwyn deserved an explanation. After all, he'd stuck with her through thick and thin and was the closest she had to a friend in the station. "If I tell you, promise to keep it quiet?" He nodded. "I won't apply for the job because I'm pregnant."

THE END

AVAILABLE NOW BY HELEN H. DURRANT

RACHEL KING
Book 1: NEXT VICTIM
Book 2: TWO VICTIMS
Book 3: WRONG VICTIM

THE DCI GRECO BOOKS
Book 1: DARK MURDER
Book 2: DARK HOUSES
Book 3: DARK TRADE

THE CALLADINE & BAYLISS MYSTERY SERIES
Book 1: DEAD WRONG
Book 2: DEAD SILENT
Book 3: DEAD LIST
Book 4: DEAD LOST
Book 5: DEAD & BURIED
Book 6: DEAD NASTY
Book 7: DEAD JEALOUS
Book 8: DEAD BAD
Book 9: DEAD GUILTY

MATT BRINDLE
Book 1: HIS THIRD VICTIM
Book 2: THE OTHER VICTIM

FREE KINDLE BOOKS

Please join our mailing list for free kindle crime thriller, detective, mystery, and romance books and new releases, as well as news on Helen's next mystery!

www.joffebooks.com

DO YOU LOVE FREE AND BARGAIN BOOKS?

Thank you for reading this book. If you enjoyed it please leave feedback on Amazon, and if there is anything we missed or you have a question about then please get in touch. The author and publishing team appreciate your feedback and time reading this book.

Follow us on Facebook www.facebook.com/joffebooks

We're very grateful to eagle-eyed readers who take the time to contact us. Please send any errors you find to corrections@joffebooks.com

YOU MAY ALSO ENJOY

Shocking family secrets come to light when a young woman is murdered

Amy Hill, a nineteen-year-old student, is strangled and her body dumped on open ground in the city. New police partners, DI Jim Neal and DS Ava Merry are called in to investigate this brutal crime. The last person to see Amy alive was Simon, the son of a family friend, but before he can be properly questioned he disappears.

Detectives Neal and Merry are led on a trail of shocking family secrets and crimes. Can this duo track down the murderer before anyone else dies? Stopping this tragic cycle of violence will put DS Merry's life at risk in a thrilling and heart-stopping finale.

If you like Angela Marsons, Rachel Abbott, Ruth Rendell, or Mark Billingham you will be gripped by this exciting new crime fiction writer.

DEAD SECRET is the first in a new series of detective thrillers featuring DS Ava Merry and DI Jim Neal. Ava Merry is a young policewoman, recently promoted to detective sergeant. She is a fitness fanatic with a taste for dangerous relationships. Jim Neal is a single dad who juggles his devotion to his job with caring for his son.

Set in the fictional Northern city of Stromford, this detective mystery will have you gripped from start to shocking conclusion.

HABIT a #1 best-selling thriller that you won't be able to put down,

A young woman, Rebecca Heilshorn, lies stabbed to death in her bed in a remote farmhouse. Rookie detective Brendan Healy is called in to investigate. All hell breaks loose when her brother bursts onto the scene. Rebecca turns out to have many secrets and connections to a sordid network mixing power, wealth, and sex. Detective Brendan Healy, trying to put a tragic past behind him, pursues a dangerous investigation that will risk both his life and his sanity. Habit is a compelling thriller which will appeal to all fans of crime fiction. T.J. Brearton amps up the tension at every step, until the shocking and gripping conclusion.

Made in the USA
Columbia, SC
21 December 2019

85415733R00140